T0068051

JACK LAW

JACK LAW

TA ROBINSON

authorHOUSE®

AuthorHouse™ UK
1663 Liberty Drive
Bloomington, IN 47403 USA
www.authorhouse.co.uk
Phone: 0800.197.4150

© 2018 by TA Robinson. All rights reserved.

No part of this book may be reproduced, stored in a retrieval system, or transmitted by any means without the written permission of the author.

First published by AuthorHouse   12/07/2011

ISBN: 978-1-4678-8003-9 (sc)
ISBN: 978-1-4678-8004-6 (e)

Print information available on the last page.

Any people depicted in stock imagery provided by Thinkstock are models, and such images are being used for illustrative purposes only. Certain stock imagery © Thinkstock.

This book is printed on acid-free paper.

Because of the dynamic nature of the Internet, any web addresses or links contained in this book may have changed since publication and may no longer be valid. The views expressed in this work are solely those of the author and do not necessarily reflect the views of the publisher, and the publisher hereby disclaims any responsibility for them.

'Good morning sir' the receptionist said in a formal manner befitting an unfamiliar gesture or welcome from the eloquently spoken, well trained temp sitting behind the reception desk wearing a perfect fit uniform, obviously, either her client knew that she would be the replacement or by some chance in a million they indeed had the uniform that fit. Anyhow she smiled as the gent returned his own rhetorical version of welcome, the normal receptionist, old George, knew the regular employees by name and he was on first name terms.

'Good morning . . .' browsing at her name tag.

'Beverly Parkson . . .'

The gentleman had the audacity to drool over the temporary receptionist as if her welcome to him was an invitation to flirt. She kept her smile up but professionally kept her gaze on the gent knowing that he had more to say.

'You sure look better than that old guy that sits there'

'Why, thank you sir' she says politely.

He was more willing to break the formality than she appeared to and detecting an uncomfortable moment developing he allowed his gaze to capture her eye and went straight for the point.

'My name is Carl . . . Carl Manning . . . please forgive me, but, Bev; you are stunning, I would be honoured if you would allow me to take you out for lunch today'

1

'Well I might have nothing planned' she kept up her guard but sounded willing to go for lunch with the presumptuous but confident gentleman, she liked his approach being straight forward and all.

The temp considered the offer and kept her gaze also, after all, she was an employee also and after work there is always time for fun and getting around.

It was typical of Carl to move in this way he was always confident and never shy around women he had the ability to create a vibe from as little as a B-minor or an augmented 7th, probably to this fact and it being the reason why A-Class Studios kept him on as an audio editor and chief sound engineer, not only did he have an ear for sound he also had an eye for the ladies.

'Ok . . . it's agreed then' she said.

Beverley pretended like it was a tough decision but she'd also made it sound like she had satisfied some curiosity that she had had, and to that end then that it would be fine to lunch with Carl, she crooned. 'See you later'.

'I will see you later' Carl Manning replied.

Manning went on through the electronic security barrier gate and on up to his studio on the 6th floor via the elevator.

His studio is decked out with a 32-bit channel mixer and all sorts of peripheral equipment and auxiliary devices. The studio itself is within his office space, he could sit outside of this thickened green tinted glass panel wall which was not only sound proofed but gave solitude from the natural world to make phone calls and do the necessary paper work or read it seems from a strange set of annuals resting on a book stand with references to Witches Covens, Ghouls and Ghost and Death, the walls were matted black even the ceiling tiles, they were manufactured using a special coating of atmospheric absorbent fibre he insisted the company utilise so that he could concentrate better when working on his projects, so, whenever Carl worked he was alone and isolated in this quiet shell and only the sound he created would be heard through the small twin

Herbech speakers mounted in the corners at 6ft 6in height above the Walend Knit black shag pile carpet. If he wanted light he would utilise two standing lamps controlled by a touch sensitive pad on the console.

It was a normal morning at the office with other work colleagues doing their chores but Carl wanted a cuppa he was fine tuning a sound of a bell but could not get it just right the clarity of the recording was distorted but he wanted to observe it as he described it the sound he wanted was mass clarity, and to the skilled ear one could observe it, he insisted on mass clarity.

Carl left his work space and went back down to the reception lobby using the elevator to spy the temp.

'Hi Bev' he was informal in his approach.

'Do you have a break?' he asked.

'Hi back at ya . . .' replied Bev.

The receptionist was bored and seemed very appreciative for the visit.

'Hold on I'll call the security guy he'll cover for me, I guess I can have a quick one'

Beverley beckoned the cover whilst she and Carl went for a coffee.

'I think I'll show you my office we can grab a coffee on the way'

Carl's thoughts were way ahead or so he thought, Bev's thoughts were way ahead of his.

'I think let us forget the coffee, I want to see what you do Carl, take me straight to your office'

'Are you kidding me . . . ?' Carl could believe his luck he knows he's got it.

'All we need is the 6th floor'

As they enter the lift Carl indicates that there is a camera above then winks to the temp, she looks even better standing up he admires her physique and long locks, he knew that the heat was set and the bitch was ready for a fucking but the elevator was the wrong place.

'Door's closing'. Please mind the doors' the onboard computer electronic voice advised them to stand clear as the doors of the elevator closed. Carl had pressed the button marked six on the podium sited in the lift lobby prompting him to use lift E.

''Tis my office, please allow me'

'Wow this is cool what do you do in there?' Bev points over towards the studio.

'That would be my studio, that is where I do most of my work, come let me show you'

Carl escorts the inquisitive starlet into the studio and closes the door behind him the ambience is immediately altered they look at each other knowing that there is not much time and just as immediate as the ambience altered so did to Carl and Bev alter their demeanour, aggressively, only the crisp hiss tenured between them the sound of material and heavy breathing could be heard as they fell to the floor it did not take long before the gyrating started they held each other tight as they grappled on the Walend Knit black shag pile carpet the passion was high and evenly matched, and so was her skirt. Carl had his woman and Beverley took the man. The heavy breathing waned and a couple of long kisses mellowed the moment down to a few short but meaningful pecks.

'Bev . . . you are so beautiful I could not wait for lunch'

'Mr Manning . . . you are so sweet I wanted you too but I'd better get back to the front desk but I need to powder my nose first'

The temp didn't need baby sitting at all she got up and left Carls office on the 6th floor and entered the lift on her own but pressed for the top floor of the enterprise. She was very sexy and would have been adored by Carl as she fixed her garments and rushed up her hair which was long and straight but is now somewhat short, curly and frizzy she pouted her lips, sighed then watched as the electro-mechanical box moved between floors. 'Door's opening. Please mind the doors' The elevator stopped at level 18 she stood back as the doors flung open to let whoever wanted to get in but there was no one the doors closed Beverley wanted the 22nd floor.

Meanwhile, Carl managed to overcome the encounter and had visited the gentlemen's toilets and was about to grab himself a coffee from a vending machine but the machine was out . . .

'Damned thing!' he put out a slight angered curse and a muted tut as he kissed his teeth. The message read.

NOT WORKING . . .

He had an alternative though; Carl could make a cup of coffee in the breakout area on level 8 it just meant a little more effort on his part. So he had decided to use the stairs. There were a few people using the canteen but after all it was about teatime.

'Hi Carl how are you? And how's it going with the sound effects?' he was interrupted by Jenny.

'Yhea, morning darling, we are nearly ready for the dubbing' Carl replies.

Carl was interrupted as he was making a cup of coffee by a couple of editors whom are working on the same project he has been working on but one of them was not so a hot blooded male as is Carl.

'Did you see that new girl at the front desk? She is real cracker don't cha think so? I would sure like to give her a good dubbing . . . ha, ha ha!' Mustafa chuckled.

Carl would not let on that he has already mixed with the temp in his studio and avoids making a crass remark in front of a female colleague the likes of Jenny but offers only to finish the sound effect, 'a.s.a.p'.

'Sure I will have it done anytime now I have just come up here for a coffee the vending machine on my floor is out. How are you doing, no need to ask you ya dumb ass can't you see there is a lady present' Carl directs his rebuttal on Mustafa.

'Hey only kidding man' Mustafa says.

'I'll kick your ass' Carl replied but he was not in the mood for Mustafa or his sad suggestive remarks.

'No, don't worry Carl but why you so protective?' Jenny asked.

'Look I just want to get a coffee and get back to work is that ok with the two of you. I will have it done right!' Having made a cup Carl was ready to leave the editors in the breakout.

'Huh, man he is short, what is his problem today? . . . Hey! . . . hey Carl by the way did you hear the news, apparently there is a space object heading directly for a collision with the earth and it is going hit somewhere later this evening . . . hey Carl you better watch yourself man' says Mustafa in a threatening manner.

Carl heads off back to his office with a cup of coffee ignoring Mustafa and leaving the team members to stew, forgetting it was quicker to use the stairs and goes round to the lift lobby only to meet a load of people waiting for an elevator.

'Whoa! What is going on here?' he asks

'Hey Carl, the lifts are stuck on 22 man' Jimmy offers an explanation

'Ok thanks I will take the stairs . . . Jimmy'

'Carl wait here's an elevator now . . . .'

'SCREEEEAAMS'

'What the . . . !!!' . . . Jesus Christ . . . !

As the lift doors opens something scares the living daylights out of those people waiting on the lift lobby area causing a great deal of commotion.

'Jesus Christ what the devil is it' Carl hurls out the question, he turns back to see what had happened a couple of women had fainted some fled and those that remained stared into the open lift in open awe shaking and filled with fear. Carl summoned up the courage to see what was in the lift, but when he peered into the open elevator there was nothing, nothing but an empty elevator.

'Look everybody, everybody look there is nothing there, is this some kind of a joke? Well it is not funny; there is fuck all in there!'

The scent of Beverley wafted by his nostrils, Carl raised his head to catch more of it.

'You know what you are all fucking mad'

Carl dismissed the incident all as a sick joke but no one was laughing at all but he tried to dismiss it as if it were a prank.

'Carl . . . . ! Carl Manning, I tell you man . . . something came out of there' assures Jimmy.

Jimmy was shaking like a leaf and whilst aiding a woman whom had passed out, he too needed assistance but Carl saw nothing in the elevator and was in no mood to believe in something he can't see, he was having none of it. The lift door closed but no one got in or out.

'I tell you man something came out of there. Something . . . something?'

Jimmy watched as Carl walked away his voice fading but Carl just headed back to his office and walked into his studio the scent of Beverly's perfume hit his nostrils again he closed the door. Immediately the ambience turned silent, he sat in his high profile leather swivel chair and reclined back ready to sip on his coffee, he had not realised that he had thrown away his coffee during the commotion upstairs, his thoughts kept returning to the temporary receptionist.

'Shit!' Carl offers the exclamation in err of what had just occurred. 'I got work to do, forget the coffees . . . fuck!' It seems frustration is the order of the day here, maybe I can go back down and see Bev . . . , no, forget that too' Her scent was enough.

Carl flicked a switch on his 32 bit mixing desk just to break the silence in the studio he played the sound track of one of his favourite movies and forgot about this need for coffee. He closed his eyes recollecting the old way how music was recorded the master tape was all important and the tape machine the spool would spin at a constant rpm round and round and round and round, the track itself was nice and easy with no singing it made him relax and whenever he was in need of peace Carl would sit at the console and flick switch 1 close his eyes and relax. He had a sudden jolt like a nervous reflex, he heard a voice say to him 'Relax back and enjoy the ride' and whilst drifting off and his thumb hit a button on the mixing board this action made the sound of the bell emit from the speakers it was the bell sample that he was working on earlier it was clear and crisp and mixed well with track. He fell into a deep sleep the sound of the bell was so crystal clear and crisp that it could be heard ringing out above the high frequencies the mix was sublime and it rendered Carl into a state of total hypnotic realms.

Traffic was heavy and slow moving . . . yet still . . . it seemed there was plenty of time to get to the Grey Lawn Cemetery and to lay those customary flowers and to conjure up that customary wry smile before entering into the twilight zone, a cortege would move slowly anyway, it is a mark of respect for the dead, you know?.

But after a long hour and the thin line between rage and calm the silver coachwork mimics the camber and the turn off point where the road meets the kerb, the driver skilfully manoeuvres the vehicle to make the car ride the verge entering the graveyard gates of the Grey Lawn Cemetery. Now begins the moment to allow the memories and silent thoughts to cloud over the highways with all its faults for now this part of the journey has now ended and the wheels come to a halt.

'Wait Here.' the instruction was abrupt but to the point.

Thoughts that would always become moulded about the face, making it appear solemn and twisted with closed mouth and tight lips wry to the cause, a wry smile, he tries never to ever forget that fallen lover the friend he adored and loved so much but had never really missed as much as he should have but for over and over and o'er the course of his own existence would soon find out how much he should have missed his lover. For when he placed that floral bloom down on the grave, surely it was not just a date that was buried there. He made an effort to leave the graveside after a while but by some strange sense, a sense of Déjà Vu maybe, he turned his head involuntary to look over his right shoulder, his body followed a full 180 degrees to settle with him looking over his left shoulder, in full focus it came, the date engraved in stone but no name and no Edith! Nor an epitaph! It should have dawned on him long ago for that matter for so and ever more to him that person laid there was more than just a date, then, out of respect and with an extreme show of tenderness he went back to the brush away the settled but ever changing earth life that settled on and even by the graveside but for that instant in time that he stood there the earth was still and would not change, only the seconds ticked by.

'OK, let's move on, for a moment there I wondered who I am'

The cab was a little dirty on the inside and in need of a good valet service, yet there was no need to complain another cab would have been just as filthy. Silver Cabs own motto reads like . . . When you need a ride remember Silver Cabs Call 02886 66534 . . . he supposed; A cab is on the road and in the busy times a good clean out was hard to come by.

He had asked for a driver who would be responsible and who knew the city where they would be going and one whom would not mind infrequent stops on the way, not much to ask, especially as a fare paying customer.

NO SMOKING . . . in big red letters was in plain sight but that did not seem to matter, fag butts and burn marks were evident some passengers would smoke on regardless, and for that matter the driver was smoking any how's as she drove, he guessed smoking a fag would be the soother that helps one to get through the hours and the long traffic queues, road rage the Give Ways and the Byways, Stop lights and signs. So after leaving the Grey Lawn he felt relieved and a little less tensed and the driver had noticed this.

It was about 19:15 in evening a balmy heat and quite a low sun for this time of year. A bright orange glow shot across the sky it could be seen between the tall buildings they themselves created a unique skyline and backdrop for the coming sunset.

'Relax back and enjoy the ride, we'll soon be there darling' the driver spoke with a typical but regular accent that fit the urban setting.

She pulled on a fag as if it were her last breath a very deep intake followed then a glance into the rear view mirror.

'Soon be there babe'

As a fare paying passenger the only choice he had really was not to take the advice offered by the cabbie.

'Excuse me Miss, could you wind down the window the button don't seem to be working back here'

'Sure . . .'

'You don't smoke huh?'

'No'

'I'll shut down the air conditioning then'

'What . . . ! No thanks'

'It will only get hotter in here! And what with all that smoke you have to be kidding . . . open the window madam'.

It wasn't much like conversation but more like a task of rebuttals going on between them. Throughout the jaunt, conversation was kept to the minimum the strange sky was more intriguing.

'Please pull over here I think maybe I'll walk the rest of the way and you can smoke yourself to death, you don't need me' he wasn't trying to be polite. His tone was slightly sarcastic.

'Suit yourself honey I don't give a shit . . . , to hell with you man! Hell to you!'

The female cabbie had become annoyed and exponentially sarcastic in return and for some ungodly or unknown reason she started shouting off abuse on the unsuspecting gentleman in the back seat of the cab.

'Look just please let me out here would you?'

The female cabbie continued with the verbal abusive rant . . .

'Your bullshit man, you are all the same if I had the strength I would kick your ass man right here right now you piece of shit'. Her lips were drying and cracking and the veins on the temple at the side of her head were full with blue blood.

She suddenly pulled up by a kerb and under poor control of her vehicle causing her passenger to fall forward towards the seat in front of him and forcing him into using his arms to break the fall, the front wheel rolled up and then off the kerb. The chrome bumper scraped the kerb stone as the car stopped, a reflection in the cloud appeared on the bumper as the dust rose up from the heap of settled earth, was this the same driver that had taken him smoothly across town.

'Oh . . . for god's sake woman!' he cried. It seemed life was back to its reality the calm gave way to rage as the impatient and tiresome attitude of the urban habitant's reticence of pent up feelings being released, but who is the one that is pent up here.

'What is your problem, here take the money and keep the change'

'You can keep your fucking money you fucking bastard! I don't want your ills you are the pits and you smell like garbage . . . to hell with you man . . .'

Ok then, he said I'll just get out here.

He had barely gotten out of the cab and set foot on the pavement when the woman cabbie drove off at a high and alarming speed with tyres screeching against the worn tarmac also, with the car door still ajar, a freak looking imp appeared to slam the car door shut, but, at a second glance the car door slammed shut because it had to, he could still hear her foulmouthed rant as she drove off recklessly hitting two other cars on the way, what a commotion. The burning rubber gave up a stench which wafted up his nostrils he stood in disbelief at what had just happened the screeching tyres silenced only by the increasing distance between him and what he could, quite rightly, describe as a maniac, ye the maniac woman cabbie drove like a bat-out-of-hell alright, and away out of sight but at first glance that imp was ugly mother whatever it was.

He didn't really need to brush the tailored suit he wore, I guess it was a nervous reaction, involuntary, but he brushed the shoulder and breast area anyway then straightened the jacket by pulling on the hem then walked the last couple of blocks to the place where he was heading. Leaving no prints on the way his light tanned Canadian moccasin paced to his detriment, he could not help but to look up toward the strange but beautiful colours the low sun had created on the nimbus stratus, at least that insidious woman driver was gone he thought and then reached into his pocket and took out an envelope containing the invitation he put in his jacket pocket before setting out. It read . . . .

SC Property and Developers

Take Pleasure in inviting

Mr JACK LAW

To the

ANNUAL GALA and AWARD CEREMONY

For the People in the Industry

At the **ELITE ROOMS**

19:00 Sharp 10/07/2018

'Can I tempt you with a drink sir or maybe something else that might take your fancy?'

A breathless gorgeous woman had meandered over to where the fellowman is standing by the entrance to the hall he had just arrived and with a cool manner and nonchalant mood was admiring the inner surroundings of the old venetian style building the old place had been completely renovated on the inside many off the original artistic features have been removed as they were irreplaceable but the architecture kept its discourse and etiquette subtle reminders of the splendid antiquity re-plastered in its place only the outer walls of stone craft and dome would remain it was built during the French renaissance period of the 16th century, it is known as the old place and so called because it is now surrounded by the new pristine steel and glass structures that seem to have sprung up all over the place and over the years most if not all the old buildings have gone to that graveyard in the dust, the building is listed and sits well inside the cosmopolitan area of Western this district though oddly named is actually east of the city centre, the decor and a spectacular lighting set made up of these huge green and blue shards neither gave up or offered no clue that this was an old place until your eyes settled upon the original mahogany panel set walls with faded areas where some old portraits must have hung but had not yet been replaced. The setting made entirely of a glass display deliberately shattered to increase the effect; much like glass fibre optics, would create an illusion, as an array of lights when angled side-on would appear to seep out of the cracks and the slight movements of the light fixtures gave off a constantly changing image and mood. The effect was sublime and would calm each of the guests as they arrive and make their entrance, it told straight away and obviously had its effect, it made those fellows relax. The glass structure was very welcoming indeed and obviously was observed by them all, the hubbub created by them whom had already metered into its luminance, fellows gathering in twos, threes and even groups it told of greater things to come.

They grazed upon the annual event like cattle, the event itself was supposedly set up to celebrate yet another year of fortunes earned from high stakes and profits yielded off the backs of the hard working labour forces people considered as working class, the real tax payers, out to make as much shekels as possible from the many hours of toil and deadlines, it is considered as work, but for the estate managers and property developers with their portfolios and fat earnings bellowing out unashamedly counted only by the by with closed deals, of course, there is nothing to worry about here though, no shame at all, the fellows are all alike even their boast could easily be compared like for like, would then vanish washed over by the waves of harrumphs emitting from these people, because these people, are the norms, man and woman, 'Fellows' alike, they are sunken deep into its bowels where each one understands the meaning of profit taking and capitalism, they are the Fellows, all in all local beings but alien to the real world of the working classes.

'I don't mind if I do' he was again comforted by the offer and accepts the offer of a drink.

'Good, then I'll have a drink at the bar with you follow me sir'. The gorgeous feline was polite and direct.

'This place is smashing, pardon the pun it was intended you know' He commented on the display with an eye fixed on the woman.

'Isn't it just' she replied. 'There is on thing worse than contemplating entering a bash on your own and that is entering the bash on your own' she said.

'That is strange I was just thinking the same thing' he said

Having just arrived and being ushered by this gorgeous feline was more than enough to make up for his thoughts; a real treat his mind was telling him also.

'He has arrived . . . let us retire to our office, we can discuss the motion at our leisure there, I have arranged a rather delightful endearing banal treat for him'

'Good, very good'

A foursome was gathered to one side of the banqueting where a huge set brown door was closed off to them he himself would not have noticed these people really but they followed his every move and were very pleased to see him and that he is now in the presents of May Flowers.

'We are sure that he has no idea who he is' a certain Shelia Charlise asks

'What if he awakes' asks Timothy cautiously.

'Well it has begun as planned and he calls himself Jack . . . Jack Law, I assure you both he will not awake' says Mitten; Carlos Mitten.

'This is very good and it is better than ever, rather exciting' says Judge Demus Trause.

'Is he going to die?'

'Good . . .' that last question was ignored. 'Let us retire to our office then, we can observe, for the truth will emit forth from him' says the Judge Demus Trause.

'Will he die?'

'That is a good question' Judge Demus Trause admits, this time the question was responded too.

'Well will he?' Shelia Charlise repeats her rather determined line of question.

'Good questions have no answers, but be it as you will the motion can only be discussed you know that Charlise, maybe you yourself would like a part to play also, does the gusto fill you Shelia?'

'I will and it does, so long as I do not succumb to the flashes then Deborah Winger will exist in me'

'Debhora Winger . . . ?' Timothy interjects

'No . . . Deborah Winger and I just made that up'

'What . . . ! Have you seen or read the script, are you party to that which has been fondled by the higher decree in this case?' Timothy has become more cautious and inquisitive and looks to the Judge for guidance.

'Oh I just made that up Timothy, tis the force of that poor soul which came to us during the fall you yourself were not there present and I actually felt her pain and the dead do not feel the tremor shook the stump tis this that I fear believe me, I can play this one, do you not know that a woman scorned is more dread than the devil itself?' Shelia spoke with contempt and belittled Timothy with the charm of, that . . . but maybe only a woman could.

'Please come let us retire to our office I feel the flashes starting, we as we exist as fellows must stay in our tent lest we fall foul of the séance, please come in and close the door now' Judge Demus Trause beckoned his pact to be with him in official state within the Elite rooms boardroom suite to observe. The three fellows with him were brought together by decree and it is this in that place that they were to meet to gather that end of the decree. The huge door opened, the light in the boardroom was dark but yet they entered, the Judge Demus Trause, Timothy Watt, Carlos Mitten and Shelia Charlise went in and sat round a great table cut from a tree stump but as natural as it fell the surroundings would be unfamiliar to any mortal soul on earth but to these fellows the brown and green but near dark blue colour hue of light below what was clearly stars in the night sky was comforting to them and gave them sight of each other but they sat looking skyward with their hands clasped tight.

A small brown door next to the large door opened and a woman walked out and closed the door behind her she melted away amongst the guest and became part of the hubbub. 'Deborah . . . ! Come here my dear how are you . . .'

Meanwhile . . .

'You can lead me anywhere darling but please allow me to introduce myself my name is Jack . . . ! Jack Law and you are . . . ?'

The well manicured gent positions himself to the lady and not really believing that she was an usherette especially with that dress she wore and said.

'I'm afraid I have not had the pleasure . . . I mean I have not met you before, I am sure I'd remember an attractive woman such as yourself'

He wasted no time in hinting that he had a liking for the woman for she had an illuminance all of her own to match that of the spectacle abode.

'So there was something else that he might fancy' she guessed

'Well Jack, follow me if you will, your name is known to me and I have been patient to meet you and I have heard so much about you'.

It was easy to melt into the flow of the linguist she was very friendly and skilled in her art of introduction.

Like a woman she just positioned her arm under his arm without even making a ripple.

'I love your Jacket nice texture, you can call me May. I bet you know a lot of these guests here tonight?'

The question was asked as part of the rhythm, the rhythm that Jack would be unaware of and at this particular juncture all of the entire guests there and fellows were hamming it up.

He allowed May to lead him the way, though he had no real choice for by now her arms were keenly entwined with his. As they walked over to the bar Jack acknowledged something quite strange, it was really strange . . . some of the guest . . . , they would appear before him lit up under the lighting system like placards, placards on show one by one, and he thought to himself that the effect was unreal but it was surreal and he became a little unnerved by it, he would only motion his eyes as if to stare but not allowing his head to really turn, he thought that May hadn't noticed them so he never looked back to justify what he saw barring the fact that he came to know each one of them somehow. He'd recognised them but couldn't tell where from. He sniggered to himself then thought, the only things missing here were the titles for each one, and he imagined that those people's names were in printed text being placed on each placard that had flashed up before him but then he remembered also the missing portraits that were not hung upon the very rich mature mahogany walled panels they had not been replaced but the named plates were still in place on the old mahogany wall panels. Jack didn't let it spook him though and shook it off thinking to himself that it was the lighting that was playing tricks on his mind but the names he thought he saw whilst going by was in fact the same names of those named plates on the mahogany panelled wall.

It didn't seem to matter to anyone nor did it occur to him that for an organisation to put on an event such as this and to exact extreme extravagance and spectacle and then for that same organisation to forgo the absents of the old portraits and just leave the bare walls in a state of disrepair should have really beggared some disbelief or even provoke comment but it didn't. It should have been mindboggling leading to inapprehension but it still it didn't.

'So, Mr Law . . . who are the four that were portrayed on the wall and why are they not hanging and gaining the respect, you know, so we the fellows could ogle them as we pass by?'

A fellow in the corridor asked a pertinent question. He was unrepentant and jovial in nature and he adds more steam to the event.

'Where is the judge why has Charlise's portrait been taken down?' suddenly more questions are being asked.

'Well as you asked my friends and so you may not wonder, then, let me tell you, I see you are wondering, but before I tell, you need to know this, I need you to concentrate on the wall, I need you to see the first and the last my friends'

A commentator offered an introduction at pace equal and jovial in nature. But he went on . . .

'Carlos Mitten, an associate member of the Fellows and Shelia Charlise MCA EEc. Timothy Watt MCA EEc (Given) and Judge Demus Trause are the founders of the Billett Society, they have power to pass judgement and the power was afforded them by the Higher Decree that sits outside the common laws of Time and Scientific laws, laws that govern the typical goings on beneath the skies. According to the Billett Society the remnants of the soul are taken back to earth whereupon the Higher Decree fondles the agreements made between the founders, a typical outcome is this, a new name is spent on the deceased person so that they do not enter a new life but they are taken even further back to a time on earth to discover undisclosed truth and because the agreement is fondled the fellows cannot pass critical comment for they do not know the result of the agreement that was fondled not until light is made dark and the sun is made low and they themselves sit like peers of a jury to witness the hearing. It is also said that lowest person that forms the founders will cross question your remnants by fire and torment until the undisclosed is made disclosed to all that are not yet made separate from the soul. Therefore woe betides he whom is found to have separated a life from a life. Again a typical outcome is this, Carlos Mitten, associate member of the Fellows agrees with the MCA EEc (Given) that an action which causes the separation of a life from a life the guilt is then multiplied ten times by the action which causes the separation of a life from a life therefore if the guilt is felt by a defendant either sole or company it is that guilt that is multiplied and fondled by the Higher Decree and so on and so on . . . This is the Law and the laws of the Billett Society and coveted the Higher Decree therefore new laws will be deemed thus plausible and necessary.

'But what of the MCA EEc that was not (Given) and the Judge?. He asks 'What happens to Shelia and the Judge Demus Trause. Please pardon my ignorance' the questions still come.

So, the commentator continues . . .

'The Billett Society and its founders have knowledge, they know that knowledge is power and they are fallen souls, they themselves turned away from the God of Man because of that knowledge they have, they have no guilt they are the wicked on the earth and their wickedness is made use of by their demented acts of passion evil doers acting the seasons of Demus Trause the fall of summer into autumn.

The Judge of what is born again when winter raises the spring and Mon Clavia Asood Eva Eva (cede) it was the song the dead sing when the sacrifice is made. Carlos Mitten read the text it was the original text scribed on the back leaf of the Book of the Dead, and the sap used to write, by the lip it was sucked up and indeed by the Judges daughter it was as an act of betrayal but she could not have known the exact ritual it was by chance it came true I tell you, Shelia Charlise used her tongue to pen it. It is them that should be hung up on the panels the old mahogany walls. Again a typical outcome is this my friends, The Higher Decree will fondle your actions that even the fellows even you do not know what you do'.

As Jack and May walked on through the glittering arena he turned to greet some other guest closest to him and one after another would greet them by shaking hands with smiles and the customary nod of the head and then the guest would congratulate themselves then continue to talk loudly and excitedly. May smiled her hellos too she was popular just like Jack a fellow in her own right.

At the bar the melody continues.

'What can I get you?' the bartender asks.

'I'll have a JD on ice . . .'

'And for the lady?' the bar tender asks

'I'll have the same . . . , a JD but hold the D!' the bartender enjoys the slight prank, even he knows Jack Law.

'I was just kidding'

In pretence she played out that she nearly let the cat out of the bag but Jack gave her a playful smile in return too, and says

'You certainly spice up what may have been a dull night' he gleamed

The cat was let out of the bag alright, but who's kidding who?

'Yhea, don't you just hate these boring events and all that wibble wobble.' She quips.

'That wibble wobble will be coming from Sir Brent Fuller.' The bartender adds.

'Oh yes Sir Brent Fuller he has a Bsc. Hons Degree and all that with eyebrows to match. But I am particularly interested in what he has to say about futures' Jack admits

May listened keenly keeping her eyes focused on Jack if there was a game to be given away she sure kept that hidden she was a professional and very charismatic.

'Your drinks', the bartender interrupts the seemingly leisure affair.

'It is the language of the dead sir . . . ! Wibble wobble . . . you know'

The bartender added his own version to the conversation and gives off a knowing wink towards his customers.

'Wibble Wobble . . . it is the language of the dead sir' he repeats

The bartender wanted to get the point of order across so that Jack could not ignore him again.

Jack hadn't a clue why the bartender heckled the point and ignored it again then received the JD's on ice from the pretentious barman and handed May her glass, it was heavy a cut glass tumbler nearly filled with the dark brown liquid and ice combination and glittering in the cool luminosity, the gentle hubbub became slightly amplified.

'Cheers' he raised his glass.

'Here's to our futures' she replies, but her thought was much different;

'Here's to our past more like . . .' the bartender continued to heckle the pair and went on to serve a couple of fellows with drinks.

'What will it be?' he asks. 'The language of the dead is not wibble wobble at all' he gladly but subtly reiterates the phrase to them.

Ha ha-ha . . . !

The barman and the fellows engage in laughter to up the ante, they continue to talk up the traits of the Billet Society and enter into discussion about agreements.

May allowed her liking for Jack to shine through this time and he couldn't help but notice the perfect lips she had.

Her lips were glossed to a very high finish definitely not cheap, a kiss was to be so tempting but would be out of place because they were not alone although it seemed they were forasmuch as from the moment May besotted Jack when he entered the bash she had literally grabbed his attention.

'Is this woman really interested in this particular annual event or was it that she is after something or someone?' Jack was trying to sum up the feline.

The thought had entered into Jacks mind so the question had to be asked thus requiring an answer and kissing those lips was a real temptation too for that thought, Jack noticed that her eyes sparkled like the cut glass tumblers given them by the bartender. Was that admiration for him? There might as well have been no one else around as seemingly for him he had eyes for her only. The heckling from the barman hadn't bothered him either.

He put a gentle hand on her shoulder then made his approach.

'I am interested to know where you operate from?' he asked, whilst sipping coolly on his drink then resting it on the bar leaving his other hand free.

She sips her drink too and puts her glass down on the bar she looks at him her eyes still sparkled but they were very wise.

'You know Jack, I have an office uptown with my partner he is over there talking with the fellows from the Civil associates and I am here talking with you I'll introduce you to him to you later . . . this is quite a bash'. She says, keeping the momentum going.

'Yhea . . . , this is a nice place and you are a real beauty May its hard to keep my eyes of you'.

Jack followed the curves of her statue; she knows that he is eying her up so she touched him on his arm flirtatiously walking her fingers down his jacket sleeve then held his hand.

'Your Hand is warm' she says 'I like a man with warm hands, with a warm hand you can have all the woman you want, drink up now and tell me what will be your next move'.

Jack did not know whether she was talking about business or pleasure but played along with the line in gesture.

'You don't waste time do you' he says.

'How about we get out of here and we go to my place where I can show you my best move'.

This was obviously the right approach it gave amnesty and to the feline starlet whose eyes squinted slightly yet sparkled like a wondrous star far off in the night sky and yet still so near spied his intent.

She moved towards him to whisper in his ear her scent was enigmatic she was also warm and fleecing she sighed with cool minted breath about his neck Jacks arm went about her waist he could feel her firm but subtle frame through the maroon blue satin and silk dress neatly clasp about her, the sigh sounded like kiss me so he did, he kissed her on her lips, she tasted like candy and again this time the kiss became now, now, meaning Jack was smitten by her undefeatable charm.

How can this be in all the glory of the evenings fair and again to find oneself embraced with a woman, and, a very beautiful woman at that and let alone the fact they had just met not even that long ago it must be the fastest speed date worthy of an entry in the Guinness Book of Records, yet the kiss is mutual and intended but were they both ready for the impact.

'I don't care about the annuals let us go now to a place more quiet'. She with even more want abound would give it up. He thought. Their suggestivity rolled between them like a magic ball and the kissing became more and more intense.

'I see you've met each other then?'

There came an interruption to that point and the demons that were broiling the stock coiled and rallied their tails like the inequities of the month of March . . . stopped their rude behaviour there and then and the barman looked over towards May he was polishing a glass tumbler and ready to serve up more drinks.

Jack and May came out of the very brief encounter after being disturbed by someone gently rubbing them both on their shoulders, another fellow perhaps, and one whom goes by the name of Deborah Winger!.

'Can I join you both . . . she paused . . . for a drink of course!?' she was quick witted.

'Of course . . . ! There came a quicker response from May. 'Debhora . . . ?'

'Deborah, my name is Deborah Winger (but I don't remember saying my name) just call me D-wing' she was impressed on how quickly her gusto was fondled and her query became a part of the observation.

Deborah raises a hand to beckon the bartender and orders the drink the bartender so verily desires to serve.

'I'll have what their having, and by the way, what's in it? She laughs.

'JD on ice' . . . Jack reveals the concoction . . . can you handle it?

The threesome gives up a slight embarrassed chortle between themselves.

The chortles became laughter it seemed everyone in the place that evening was laughing and bordering on ravenous behaviour, not unlike revelry.

'Oh Jack I don't know what came over me you seem to be quite a man'.

'May you are more than quite a woman'.

Jack wanted it to go on, was it her eyes, her luscious lips that did the trick, the feel of her statue or was it something even more intoxicating anyhow none of the other guest paid them any mind the hubbub carried on relentless and the occasional raised voices and laughter could be heard all about, after all this was a money orientated field where big deals are to be spun and even bigger stories will be told.

He was still under her spell and mesmerised by the sparkles in the woman's eyes and offered for one more purse on her pouted lips, the gloss only but slightly tainted, to finish of the moment . . . ,

. . . It takes a professional to know how close a meeting . . .

May raised her hand exposing her palm toward Jack.

(This is the international signal for STOP). When the effect is created by a female it really does mean stop and no more.

. . . Well, maybe in this case the meeting is sure to convene and very soon . . . Jacks thoughts were running away with him.

'Let me introduce you' May carries on with the effect, she was really quite joyful that her friend had turned up.

'This is Debhora Winger . . . , Jack, we call her 'D-Wing' for short, **she be the one** . . . !' she paused then corrected herself. May Flowers had quickly learnt about her friend and was nonethewiser but for Deborah Winger the transient apparel was instant all she had to do was be there for now. It was that question that she asked which provoked the Higher Decree to promote her part . . . 'Is he going to die . . . ?'

May continues . . .

'D-wing is the one, who has told me all about you Jack, and she was spot on sir, you really are the magnificent character as described in the (OPM) Own Property magazine' The OPM, is a popular magazine read by the real estate managers and developers alike the magazine runs features and interesting articles for the industry . . . of course . . . like land and mining, building and construction and that sort of thing and May for her part she poured out her admiration on him to flatter the man into submission, and used the opportunity well to gain her intention, well, to sort of reveal her intention also but she kept her words to just that submission that is what she wanted. She became flustered and a bit blushed but was it at the apparent ease at which she gave up the pretence and let her feelings go so easily, or maybe was it that she had feared of something else. The bartender stood in the background behind the bar looking on and observing the felines actions he raised a glass up to the light looking through it into the light before lowering it then started to polishing it energetically.

'Come on May pull yourself together' D-wing says

D-Wing had noticed the barman he seemed frustrated, but carried on with her instruction to May.

'The evening has barely begun and you Jack can you take you hands of her'.

D-Wing had the audacity to get between the pair so she can take control of what happens next.

'Shall we take our drinks to the table the dinner will be served shortly? . . . Jack . . . you can sit with us if you don't mind my editor will not be attending tonight so you can, if you will, sit with us and we can share business interest at my table'

D-Wing actually runs the OPM and covered some of the aspects of a recent refurbishment venture Jack managed through to completion acting as the project manager.

'Well thank you very much' he says, then he admits 'The pleasure is all mine'

Not only had he stepped out on his own he is now in the company of these two women.

'Not bad huh, and ready to eat', Jack amuses himself at the expense of his new find and doing some heckling of his own as he walks past a fellow and spying the bartender.

May Flowers was feeling content herself she had won the day and she felt confident that the demure character, the bachelor the guy that she has waited patiently to meet is now just a few feet away within her grasp and no matter how grown up you are, sometimes you are always reminded of the things that you want you just can not get and the things you get you just do not want. But not this time though, Jack will get away with what he wants because what he can get she is going to give it to him. The thought echoed around her head.

A waiter passes out the menu whilst another suggests wine from a wine list for the meal. Now he knows that he is no connoisseur of wine but that it would be of his choice that the ladies would desire of him but the waiter with the wine list and like all waiters is very tenacious.

'May I suggest sir?' the waiter with his nerve points to a name from the wine list.

The shadow of the waiter's index finger moves across the list straight to a foreign entry meeting with the knuckled hand with well but rather oddly manicured nails and the finger of what could be considered as possessed by the waiter. That finger appeared to belong to a much older person and does not fit the hand to which it is attached and although this waiter was aged in his own right he definitely doesn't appear that old. The waiter whom was tapping at the wine list menacingly and frustratingly, the fingernail filed to a point, obviously a point intended for Jack to choose the wine that he is pointing to with his ill looking finger.

Jack Law took the hint and agreed to the fine wording edited on the well worn wine list.

'Maybe I will try the discriminating degree of taste in a bottle of Duo Vin la Marle from the region of Je Crois rever Mouille Vallee. Translated it would mean The Wettersham valley. Jack did not speak this language and made no query about the wine or its origin or region, so as not to show up his own ignorance or to offend the aged waiter he thought would be knarred at the refusal. His thought's returned to cab driver and to how easy the she flew of the handle the bottle of Duo Vin la Marle from the region of Je Crois rever Mouille Vallee read impressively enough to him.

After a short dull moment the waiter returned with the wine, it was a very dark bottle, judging by the makers stamp, fashioned by some ancient bottle maker but the date was unclear though, an oak tanned label was affixed to it with golden coloured lettered words embossed on the label this would suggest that the wine had a good vintage.

'Shall I pour sir?'

'You may' jack announced, poking a little fun at the waiters expense.

Jack upped the anti and would speak in a posh tone but the waiter was full of it he could not be more pompous if he tried.

Like an artist at work the waiter set about popping the cork to begin the effusion.

With a couple of squeaks out came the cork with a pop the wine was poured out and at that familiar sound . . . tot tot tot tot tot-

(You can make this sound by pressing the tip of the tongue on the roof of your mouth then pulling the tongue away with lips slightly open).

-It was a superb red but for some unknown reason May broke away from her conversation with D wing only to look toward Jack their eyes met as the waiter had poured the wine into a glass for Jack to taste.

'Is the wine to your satisfaction sir?' the waiter waited quite impatiently on Jack Law.

Judging by the expression on Jack Law's face the wine was shocking to taste at first.

The wine had a burnt aroma the dark burgundy tint reflected the image of the woman sat opposite he kept his eye trained on her as he swirled the wine in his mouth then swallowed it; the wine became complex and complicated and played his taste buds like the fizz form a sherbet sweet and brought about a shiver as it went down, a strong after effect which gave a warm but unsatisfying sense of relief as the fuel became depleted.

'Sir . . . does the wine meet your satisfaction?' the pompous waiter was even more galactic in his manner.

Jack Law peered into the glass a second time this time with a cringe he sees the reflection of a man a reflection that was different than his, he raises the glass up again to his mouth to finish the sample but then refused a second experience.

'Ugh . . . ! That was ghastly . . . the wine is burnt!' Jack blurted out. The response he gave was that of shock, irksome and yuk even. And taking his attention away from May and towards the waiter giving him his full attention, he says.

'No way . . . ! That wine is not to my satisfaction at all' Jack refuses the bottle then wishes to select a wine of his own choice. It didn't matter about causing a scene or upsetting the old rag of a waiter as long as that bottle of Duo Vin la Marle from the region of Je Crois rever Mouille Vallee or, what-ever-you-want-to-call-it, was taken away.

'Are you alright' D-wing enquires of Jack?

The waiter goes off in a hump with the bottle of plonk.

'Agh . . . No! D, that bottle . . . the wine . . . is off; I . . . think . . . I'm . . . err. I'll be OK in a minute'

Jack Law was stuttering like a person whom could not put two words together then resigned to the effect that the effusion was having on him.

They would eat first then the after dinner speeches would be made and the guest would look forward to the main speaker of the evening . . . Sir Brent Fuller. As Jack was trying to pull himself together unknowing that he had now lacked the senses to even control his thoughts he had started to drift it seemed to him like he was at a cabaret or some kind of theatre show the speaker stood on stage with these huge eye brows the dinner suit was like that of a master of ceremony or maybe a circus master in charge of an elephant wowing an audience with his entre.

Ladies and gentlemen I know conjure up the main event of the evening, a drum role and cymbal crash brought about huge laughter from the audience, but seriously ladies and gentlemen it is now time for the main event and the speech we have all been waiting for, the ceremonial master waved a wand and puff of smoke billowed up from the stage along with star spangled lights that glittered as they rose upward toward the bright spot lights hanging precariously from what appeared to be from a scaffold frame setting high up toward the night sky it was the moon though that could be made out as the smoke and glitter dissipated into the air but where has the fucking dome gone or the roof for that matter back down on the stage stood Sir Brent Fuller it was him all the time he showed off his eye brows to the waiting fellows sitting in a glittering arena rolling them up and down and then the left eye brow only he would raise up eyeballing Jack as he sat watching the show.

Sir Brent rolled up his sleeves and started his oration to his audience.

'It has been a good year folks and I am honoured to be here for this magnificent gala what a spectacle indeed we should all be honoured because today we have amongst us a very distinguished fellow. His voice basses and rocks the fortification sending shivers around the body as he speaks the first line of approach. Brent continues . . .

'But first let me praise the juveniles and the cherubim's that walk behind us and follow our footmarks which we have set upon this planet, it has been our playground you know, and indeed we have played well, we never let nor do we allow them to walk beside us for we are the set that must be kept to our trade lest woe unto us, keep them apart from us as we take back what is demented to us for years and time, yes, time can never keep what is demented to you from you also for it is this that bonds us as fellows, because of the final agreement of the Higher Decree, and when anger befalls ye he that suffers for its fate will surely know he has did ye wrong yhea and all that he has done wrong he shall pay for his fortune he will pay for it with forfeit of his soul his life has never been his and I will deliver his heart to you a promise is a promise is it not? bring down the pillar of the gentiles kick the balls of their masters let them suffer to emit what fate befalls that fellow who cheats on his fellow brethren this cloven will sit in silence so that the deaf do not feel left out when the punishment is reeled upon him wipe you grief in his face and tear out his rib also, is this not how it started'.

Sir Brent Fuller used the moment to enact the beginning of a judgement. To the observer it must be remembered that when an agreement is made by the society it will then occur that the agreement is then fondled so that the act of the judgement is not known to the society and Sir Brent Fuller was majestic and to the unsuspecting quite mystical and when he revealed the fate of an unjust fellow it was just that, that fellow should be punished. His narration came in part from a paragraph written up by the Billet Society. Jack could not work out whether the speech was in celebration of successful year or a sermon by a crazed vicar or a judge summing up a case and opening a trail of a criminal. The drool became drowned out by Huncho Del Paraades and the Bandits from El Paso, it was unusual though for the entertainment to start playing whilst the main speaker was still on his feet but it had the desired effect usually there would be an ovation of some sort, but it kept the hearts beating and the pulse was vibrato.

Whilst Jack sat listening to the tirade he had become spellbound and he was not feeling at all one hundred percent but quite unlike himself , the evening carried on as normal with food being served only a different waiter would return with the new bottle of wine chosen by Jack. They ate quail in mange tout for starters with a main course rainbow trout wrapped in roasted basil leaves with honey coated spring vegetables, coffee and cognac's.

The music played on in the background creating a party-like atmosphere, an ambience all its own the music had a beat similar to the Latino Bella or La Dolce Vita grounded with hard Cuban melodies, guitars and two strange men with bandoleros on their heads waiving maracas dedicating to the art of the rhythm and three dancing girls all dressed in garments he considered to be like maybe16th century outfits wearing black buckled shoes . . . but white socks! . . . that's right but it was hard for him to envisage.

It should have been a great fortune to be sat with the two women but his feelings were that enmities existed, what were they talking about when he sampled the wine but having eaten with fine opulence and serenaded with great music still something was wrong, something was wrong with Jack, sweat started to appear on his forehead and he was more than a little uncomfortable, his stomach was revolving and his head swirling with a slight ache here and there an urgent need to lie down was the order. Jack became haunted by enmities and it showed.

'Jack, are you alright?' Deborah inquires again of him. 'Are you ok?'

'No, D . . . I'm . . . ere, ere!' Jack tried to respond but he could not he felt that he was being strangled by the neck' he then imagined a man of Caribbean origin hanging on the mahogany panel wall with a ligature round his neck.

'Jack, what has happened to you your voice, you are not making any sense' May, though, she wasn't quite as concerned for him as she might be, but instead, she puts on a good deal of emphasis that he looked like a man that was hung by the neck for the deceit, rape and murder of an entire family.

'I struggle to . . . to remember a name but that Face . . . it is him . . . god . . . .' she couldn't recall the man's name so she let it go.

'Debhora.' . . . she says, 'I think he looks quite ill maybe we should call him a cab.

'OK . . . you are a cab Jack!' D-Wing has a sense of humour even at a time like this.

'. . . Help me get him out of here' May paused but was a little annoyed at the quip.

'May my name is pronounced Deborah not Debhora . . . I will call Silver Cars now'

'No! No! Not Silver Cars please' his voice barely made impact.

He fears that he might get that wretched driver that took him to the Grey Lawn, and, if it were that female cabbie again, gods forbid. The thought was worse than the ailing mound he was suffering; it would also be no good trying to explain to the ladies what had happened they would not understand anyhow the strength he did not have.

Although seated at the table he was really unable to support himself and slumps forward onto his arm as he rested his elbow on the table knocking over his glass which he had not touched spilling the contents his other arm involuntarily came up to form full head support.

'Oh my God . . . he's going to pass out.' Deborah says

The guest sitting at the other table looked on without interest.

'Ugh . . . I feel terrible . . . man' . . . 'what the . . .' Jack reveals a lament has started.

Jack tries to come to terms with the feelings his eyes reddened and face dry skinned and pale with dishevelled hair reminiscent of the Jackal and Hyde saga, he stood up on his own two feet but was very unsteady on his own he rocked back and forth.

'I have got to get out of here now right now, what the . . . !' he points to a black man hanging by the neck on the stage where Sir Brent Fuller stood to give his speech, but only he sees it.

Other guest just looked on not really offering aid or assistance the Huncho Del Paraades and the Bandits from El Paso band played on with the pulsating beat.

'Jack wait, I am coming with you' May stopped him as she rushed to help him.

The commotion gathered more attention.

'Please help me with him!' pleaded May;

'I can't carry this man on my own' she gave a stern look at the diners sitting at the table opposite, Mann Corp a firm of solicitors joined by partnership she disrupted the conversation that they were having they were deep in discussion about the outcome of an agreement that was fondled by the Higher Decree.

'Come on let us get away from here, he is drunk' one says

Two fellows immediately got up from off their seats and moved away from the table where the group of five were sat, a man and two woman fellows remained seated they ate well too and were having a whale of a time but the fellows that remained seated showed their annoyance at the impromptu intrusion it was obviously not appreciated the two fellows that got up not only did they move away from the table but walked off and over to the lounge area beckoning the others on the way the three got up and left the dining area no help was offered.

'Take him to the outside to the fresh air it might help him to recover more quickly come on I'll help you'. A fresh faced Intern comes to assist. 'I am not a fully fledged fellow here so I can help him the rules of the society cannot stop the intervention of fate by non signed up members'

The fresh faced Intern gave enough support to Jack as he helped May Flowers to get him out to the fresh air and she was very grateful.

'Please allow me to introduce myself'

'My name is Carl . . . Carl Manning . . . !'

As they walked out of the dining area the Band played louder preventing May to actually hear the young Intern so she didn't hear the name as the fresh faced Intern introduced himself, they walked past the bar and through the lounge area and past the gallery past the glass display on the way he noticed the portraits on the rich mahogany panels and like any portrait they stared back at him the hubbub had started to increase to even greater amplified levels even enough to drown out the now insignificant but brilliant sounds created by Huncho Del Paraades and the Bandits from El Paso Band other fellows were leaving the dining area, themselves, acting like bandits also and heading for the bar and lounge to gel amongst the green shattered glass displays Jack was only one to eager to get out of there.

The efficiency at which the fresh faced Intern dealt with the ensuing situation was swift he led May and her companion to the exit and out onto the street.

May turned to thank the gentleman who had helped her out but he was gone so she wasn't satisfied that she hadn't thanked him enough and feeling that she never knew his name was even more a disappointment for her she found herself alone with Jack and that blast of fresh air he so much needed came as a welcome relief. Inside during the commotion she had asked D-wing to order a cab.

D-wing had ordered the cab for May using her Tokiax RI . . . a sleek mobile communication device . . . she gained the attention of May and signalled to her using the fingers of her right hand and clenched fist the first signal was the four fingers and thumb and following this two more times indicating 15 the rest she had to lip read.

Outside Jack was feeling a little better if not a lot better and able to put more reasonable words together, the fresh air had opened his sinuses.

'What the hell happened in there one minute I was fine and the next'

'Do not stress yourself I will get you home, she interrupted. Let us walk a bit. It will do you good'

'I'd love to walk with you' acknowledged Jack 'but I feel so deep in this thing this is so strange, I have never been this side of a woman before is this what being vulnerable feels like'

'There is a cab on its way and it will be about 15 minutes D-Wing says'

May resisted from revealing her thoughts to Jack she could see that he was in need of more strength and was not yet ready for her but she played her part and he, he would do as the feline suggested anyway, but she wanted him to be ready for the submission.

The balmy evening air struck him and the mint of her voice was like a relief train delivering much needed supplies.

'How do you feel to walk, come take my arm I will support you'

Once again Jack finds himself being led by the woman he had only met that evening but he trusted her he had no reason to distrust her.

'Lead the way I am all yours'. He says.

'Maybe the food was to rich' Jack did not consider the wine though.

'We shan't go too far now it is better for you to stand if you are feeling giddy' she says, typical of a mother caring for a child recovering from a fall.

'You have a kind nature May . . . good thing you were here with me and I feel so comfortable with you' he continued.

'And I with you Jack' May was playing the ideal partner almost too nice to be true in fact this moment was hers to cherish.

'Look I do not really know what came over me back there, feel quite a fool' he says

'That is good it means you are coming back to your senses darling you gave me quite a fright'

'That was quite a fright for me too; I have never past out before.'

'Come let us turn back our ride will be here soon' she says being in full control of the fellow, 'I think I want to take you home now, let us not go back to the annuals, but let me take you home if only I . . .' she paused.

'Say no more May, I will not let you take me home at all this is wrong I think if you are willing then I will take you to my home, now, it is my turn to lead you lady' Jack Law was near his best as he tried to turn on the charm.

'Thank goodness you are ok' she replies

The vibration mused between them was like one of pure mutuality.

'Where have you been all my life May? I have never felt so comfortable with anyone like this before and If you like my place then, you will be more than welcome to spend the night'

'Don't you worry I am sure I will like your place don't forget I have heard all about you Jack'

As they both turn about toward the way they came the cab was there waiting as if like magic.

Jack opened the door of the cab for May to get in he admired the way she slid into the waiting car she was perfect he sure felt a lot better now the gorgeous woman was his for the night and by the looks of things for an eternity.

As she sat down she gave a glance toward him indicating that she was secure he shut the door and walks confidently around to the door on the other side of the cab and lets himself in and sits down next to her before closing the door he instructs the driver to . . . 'Drive on to number 10 Delaware Avenue' and says, 'when you get there you cannot miss it, it has a glossy black door with silver lettering'

He closes the door gently, inside the cab has a fresh and clean odour and the seats were warm.

'Nice ride'

The driver peered back at him via the rear view mirror but says nothing.

'I mean the car; I was referring to your car sir'

'Thank you sir, I know that'

'Delaware Avenue it is sir'

'Yes please driver'

The driver would only peer at him via the rear view mirror. He puts the car into gear and manoeuvres away with a real smooth automatic glide.

Jack had to peel himself away from the mirror realising that he was looking at nothing the driver was now in full control of the journey and no longer talking to him or looking into the mirror.

Jack was for a moment far away but remembered May was there she was quite relaxed and just sitting there next to him.

Jack took her hand to show how much he cared for her too he was pretty much appreciative of how she had just taken control of the situation when he felt ill.

'You know May, back there seems so far away now and it is just you and me May'

She would only glance back at him with a look that would melt a ferocious beast the air had given her a new chance to glow and her beauty shone through.

'You certainly have the good fortune and the looks, you're beautiful' Jack says to her but he could not help comparing the cab to the one in which he had taken earlier. The journey back to his place was quicker the traffic queues had died down and indeed the sun was now set, set down below the horizon, the banter between them was short not much was said May sat back and allowed her hand to do the talking she held his hand tightly throughout the journey.

Once back at his flat the mood was a little timid and an uncertain discomfort had crept in so Jack offered to make his new guest a drink.

'I love coffee would you like one or maybe something a little stronger?'

'Oh coffee would be fine' she says

'A little music., Jack reached for his music system remote control then selected an album compiled from movie sound tracks the TV came alive showing scenes of rolling hills and valleys but no sound. 'I will just dim the lights, if you like the shower is right through there on the left'

'Jack you have a lovely place it is really cool here a shower sounds great . . . will you join me'

'Ok . . . I have started the percolator' just like a true gentleman jack always humours his girlfriend.

'Oh Jack I think this is going to be the start of something great please let us hold each other under the shower and just let the warm water wash over us'

She then slipped up the hem of her dress to reveal the fashionable holdup tights the blue dress she removed letting it fall to the floor her heels moored on his rug as she took them off, Jack admired her greatly.

'I hope this is the moment what you have dreamed of May let us start on a clean sheet' Jack words were spoken so as not to let May hear what he said but spoken to reassure himself. He was truly falling in love with her and she seemed innocent.

The mood moved from the shy reality to one of true knowledge one of knowing and caring to one of togetherness the moment was mutual and each knew what the other felt and wanted for the time they had together they held each they held each other as the warm water washed over them a beautiful moment was shared and May took that opportunity to fulfil a missing moment in her life her passion was deep and soulful and just to hold and caress was enough to fill that gap . . . it was done.

'The coffee taste good'

Jack and May sat together on the sofa listening to the sound and watched the views of the countryside.

'This is so beautiful I wish I could stay in this position for ever' May spoke from the heart the liking for this man the chance was a jackpot and she won admitting to herself that her appointment with the Billet Society was in fact out-of-this-world but this felt real. May tended to her man like a caring lover she gave him a cool drink which she rustled up from the cooler and added a little content of her own. Jack never really had the chance to find out why May was so relaxed, caring and loving his usual affairs were normally evident but this one will prove a challenge.

'I'll just make myself another coffee and sit with you a while just relax' she spoke with soft assuring tones and allowed her subtle frame to mesmerise him she knew he watched and that is what she preferred.

'Sure make yourself at home . . . babe' he says . . .

Jack fell asleep before he could finish his sentence he was out like a light that content she gave him was deliberate she gave him a poke to test whether he was really gone just to satisfy herself.

It seems May Flowers has achieved what she had set out to do, the conniving bitch, satisfied she made her way into his bedroom she pulled the sheets back then went back over to the sofa, somehow she rustled up the strength to carry Jack she lifted him up and over her shoulder like a fireman and carried him to the bed and dumped him on it like a sack.

'I have got you now!' she smirked and laughed to herself.

She removed his gown and then the gown that adorned her own slithering body and flicked the elastic of her Sophia knickers, looked at Jack then waved her index finger with a sideways motion of her head. The perfect manicured texture of her nails even to the sleeping male was tempestuous, her matching bra then follows.

'You are not getting this beauty you bastard!' she said, she then climbed onto his bed almost cat like but purposeful the hunter and the prey. May would cuddle up to Jack and playfully rubbed up her almost naked body against his and gave his cheek a smacker, then said . . .

'Sleep tight my darling, sleep tight.

She then laid herself to sleep; leaving the lights on but dimmed —Mood Lighting—controlled by a programmed switch on a consol next to an arched opening. Jacks home had few doors the setting was very much open plan this would have set the mood for nights of passion.

There could have been nothing new about the morning bar the fact that it was the morning after the night before but then again the atmosphere could be observed if only he had the urge to observe it or is he alone in his mass of clarity in which he is to find himself this very morning.

Jack's thoughts were complex. He awoke and looked around his room it appeared that there was a scene to be admired he saw a blue dress strewn on his Moroccan Berber rug, he attained it whilst on a venture to the Medina it had had many spirits but it was the local Souk that held the item it caught his eye, he offered 2000 dinar to the trader, but immediately the trader said . . . no, no, no, with an accent fit for a Maghrebi colloquial sounding individual . . . You tell me your price and I tell you my price . . . 20000 dinar' after a drawn out session of haggling Jack paid 5000 dinars for the rug. It was as clear as crystal and seeing the dress on the rug made him feel like a conqueror if not anything else. Mays stilettos were still moored up against it, I am still alive. The trap of his lover was just that a trap, May wanted him to feel as though he had conquered her the feel of her Sophia underwear ignited his ego.

As Jack Law awakes from his slumber and contends that he had not a care in the world and after what he could consider to have been one hell of a night is also a relief to awake and find himself lying there and living, opposite to the bronzed skinned attraction that adorns his space. He thought to himself also, whist admiring her exposed torso, how the glare created by the shimmering light beams pointed outward in all directions, his girl is the home of the sun and full of life. He leans over to her and puts a hand toward the glowering and extinguishes the light show with his hand then whispers to her.

'Got to go babe' it hadn't occurred to him that he actually fell asleep in the sofa or how for that fact that he has awoke in his bedroom lying down next to May Flowers.

'OK, take care darling' she just managed to put three words together.

They acted like lovers how strange, not even the question of, did we' or how was it for you, not even an embarrassed giggle was offered by the woman and Jack for that matter played the dotting lover she wanted him to be, however her vibrations had put the spring into his step and Jack felt little resistance to head up a new day and get ready for another day in the office he rises from the bed with a swift bound almost like a leopard only this leopard has two feet and into the bathroom intending to take a look at himself in the mirror.

'May . . . what happened to the mirror it's all busted?'

'What?'

'The mirror . . .'

'Forget it . . . I'll get it fixed' the buzz he had nothing mattered.

'I'm tired darling come back to bed' she feigns.

A hint of self satisfaction adorns his expression and a glint in his eye reveals admission that he has more than lust for May, but in the shower he lets the warm water run over his body from head to feet if it was rain an umbrella seller might as well pack up and retire. He wanted to be wet and very wet.

But there was something new, for strangely his mind was filled with it, he recalled a day of a much earlier era when thoughts of a child enters his mind he sees this boy but it could be that of a young girl of an age about ten years old wearing shorts and a grey school cap, a dark coloured blazer over a white shirt displaying a motif on the upper breast pocket playing in a field amongst the hedges and bushes it was a bright day with clear blue skies and there was no one else around and yet he recalls the child was content to be there, Jack continued with the day dream in the shower which beholds him, but yet again his thoughts returned and still with the child who had then turned about and appeared to look straight into his eyes just like his lover did and like a child caught doing mischief ran and hid behind the bushes out of view! . . . now Jack, who is still in the daydream seeing this through his eyes looked up and over to the right like a cameraman panning his camera lens saw the child again but this time the child was peeping through a narrow gap in a fence, but before he could see any more he was disturbed and awoken by water from the shower which had gotten into his ear bringing him out of the trance like state.

He felt it really strange though, to have had such a vivid recollection of this particular day or the child for that matter but it passed. As the warm water of the shower became the reality again he could only remember that he is on a mission and the light of day as it shone outside his home gave him a greater sense of a reality. He let the daydream pass from him.

He was a cool guy that had everything, everything like all the latest Mod-Cons and high tech gadgets at hand and a very beautiful woman in his bed, in his early forties he was smart and succeeds in his career and like the car he rides not flash or boastful but vintage with chrome bumpers he has the edge to be on top but you will have to dig deep very deep to find an flaw on this man Virgo's or any other star sign for that matter will be amazed at the figure he cuts a figure that leaves little to be desired. When asked by the many woman whom had a liking for Jack what sign he falls under Jack would reply I don't read the stars, gazing is for those with wishes my fantasy is you lady. Jack woos them and seduces them with lyric.

Before he leaves, Jack hovers over May as she lay scattered on his bed and kisses her on the forehand and admired her firm breast then leaves the room walks down the hall towards the door he failed to notice another mirror that was busted he sneezed as he passed it triggering flashes the effect when the optic nerve is pressed up against the retina he opens the front door then closes it behind him entering the outside the air is fresh despite the city glue that usually sticks around after the revelry of the night before and the days to come, yet there is no one else around, strange though, one would expect that others would be out and about or on their way to work also but it was quiet and very silent.

Ring, ring the melodious tones emit from Jacks mobile communication device a Tokiax ri

The word . . . (WITHHELD) . . . appears on the dialup window Jack is muted by this and wonders who it was calling and with his attention off the road and not looking where he is going he bumps into a woman a woman city type.

'I beg your pardon madam' he offered. 'But where did you come from?'

She did not smile but stared into his eyes with extreme annoyance she entranced him, Jack motioned the phone towards his left ear, all the time transfixed with the woman as she passed him by, Jack almost stood still but facing the wrong way he returned toward his route to continue on.

'Hello, Hello morning Mr Law'

'Ah er, er morning to you Madam' Jack replied into the phone.

'Er how can I help you er Miss . . . ?'

'It is more like, how might I help you, but you do not require my name yet'

'Well Miss whoever you are how did you get this number and how do you know my name?'

'Mr Law you do not require that information either'

Her rebuttal flexed Jack to an involuntary sideways nod that made him look outward and suddenly there were people around, like, normal, because normally there would be men, women, going about their business but Jack couldn't help but notice this woman over the other side of the road for it was the same woman whom he had just bumped into.

'What . . . !'

Jack uttered not realising he was speaking into the phone but he was referring to the woman over the road, he moved the phone into view then looked to seek out the woman again but she had gone disappeared into thin air in a split second she was gone.

'Mr Law are you still there?'

He heard the tiny voice coming from the phone and then slowly motioned the phone towards his head to listen.

'Mr Law are you . . .'

'Yes . . . he paused . . . Yes I am here but there is something really . . .'

Jack interrupted the caller, and then he usurped himself.

'Look I don't know who you are but just what is it that you think you can do for me?' his demeanour failed him and unlike his usual calm exterior repose he became defensive.

'Good, now that I have your attention Jack . . .'

He continued to walk on but was irritated and waited impatiently toward his destination as the caller enlightened him to the cause of the call.

'I will see you in your office if you do not mind . . . ? You are on your way to work are you not?'

'Yes' replied Jack eager to learn of the nature or business of the call, he repeated . . . 'Yes I am in fact I am on my way there now and I will look forward to meeting with you however mysterious all this is'.

Jack hung up the phone before the woman could say another word or so he thought.

'I will be there at 10:00am'.

Jack heard the voice clearly and swiped at the left side of his head as if to rid himself of a pesky mosquito but he knew what he had just heard.

'Pull yourself together man can you not look where you are going'.

His reaction was enough to annoy an oncoming gentleman.

'What the hell is going on?' 'What is wrong with me?' Jack spoke out in earnest of his plight then looked at the man and then said. 'I am sorry . . . I am very sorry'.

The man just walked off leaving Jack in a tidy mess.

On his way to his office Jack would usually stop off at Ruby's coffee shop this is where he would meet up with friends who liked to drink coffee and share titbits but today Jack went in ordered his usual and made for a quiet table.

'Your quiet today darling' inquires Ruby

'Oh Yes.'

'Morning Jack'

'Oh Tom didn't see you'

'Mind if I join you Jack?'

'Suit your self man, take a seat Tom'

The coffee lady walked up to Jacks table with his usual drink.

'Not quite yourself today huh babe what is the matter one to many last night'

'Just put the coffee down Ruby'. Jack's frustration ensues at Rubies blatant intrusion into his current affairs.

'Oh Ruby I will have a fresh orange juice to go with that'

Tom pulls up a seat at Jacks table.

'Jack, in the property world how is things?'

'Tom if you don't mind I just want to sit here and take it easy right now'

'What is the matter you man you look like you have seen a ghost and you are all sweaty man . . . If you ask me you need to leave it alone'

Ruby breaths down his neck . . .

'Yes, settle down and find yourself a wife'. Says Ruby as she went off to get the orange juice flirting herself knowing Jack is watching her fine arse.

Jack tried to ignore the banter ensued at his expense hoping that they would get the message and leave him alone.

'Well I'd be seeing you got to go man'

Tom left Jack pondering the events of the morning in his mind there wasn't much conversation anyways.

Ruby returned with the orange juice and sees Tom about to leave.

'Here is your juice Jack, I hope you like what you see, you going already Tom'

'I'll see you around Ruby' Tom replied

Tom waves to the pair of them but has an unsure glance towards Jack. He wonders to himself, where be his head at.

Ruby was trying to get Jacks attention with her perfect form but there was no chance of that either today, Jack kept picturing in his mind the strange woman whom he had bumped into earlier it was as if he could see right through Ruby and out onto the street.

'Who is that . . . ?'

Jack sees the woman again this time she is staring at him from across the street.

'Who is that woman . . . ?' he repeats

'Whoa steady on tiger you act like you have never seen a woman before'

Ruby turned to see what had attracted Jack out the window across the street.

'What woman Jack what are you talking about?'

Jack looked at Ruby and says

'Oh what t e hell, Look . . . !'

He pointed out across the street then realised that no one was there.

Jack had a resigned look about him and said . . .

'I think I had better go'

'Wait you haven't had your drinks yet'

No I, Jack hesitated he wanted to leave but had no idea where he was really going. James Wooten entered the coffee shop and filled it with his enormous frame.

'Morning all' the big man bellowed.

James ran a local estate agent in the nearby town just outside the city area of Western, Wooten & Struttclyde, though Struttclyde was never really seen yet all countryside and exclusive property and investments would pass through him. Struttclyde is an expert realtor.

James Wooten's size would attract everyone's attention as he strode up to the counter to order a coffee. James looked around and saw Jack and Ruby over by a table, Ruby was trying to calm Jack and to make him relax.

'Hey Jack how you doing? He strides over to where they are at Jacks table.

'Can I join you, excuse us Ruby if you do not mind I need to . . . to talk to Jack about some business, bring me an Americano will you'

'Sure anything as long as you can make him snap out of it' says Ruby.

'Snap out of what?' ask James.

'No I am ok I am fine Ruby thanks you look great'

Ruby studied Jack for a second or two and said, 'you do not look fine to me' and went to assist a good looking couple waiting impatiently over by the counter.

Jack stood up and offered his hand to the huge gentleman for brisk handshake.

'James how are you take a seat'

'How is Struttclyde?'

'Oh he is well and business is a little slow you know with the world financial markets in turmoil, bear markets and foxes, snakes and ladders but I don't want to bore you with all that bull pardon the pun'. Both men share a laugh.

Ruby admires Jack from a distance.

'I cannot stay long with you Jack but a little bird assures me that that property you enquired of some weeks ago has been sold and is no longer on the market'. James language was always like a spoonful of sugar that would go well with a bit of bad news but the message was always clear.

'Now Jack listen to me Struttclyde and myself met with the vendor of the property and also the buyer despite the fact that the sale of the property was handled by some, er somewhat unknown agent I must say' . . . James became a little unsure and his rhetoric retarded. Jack watched as James eyebrow shot upward and downward. He continued . . .

'However' James says . . . but pausing as he speaks.

'Spherewell Housing Ltd. Never heard of them, anyhow we met at the property it was a rather unusual meeting and I felt like I was been leant upon by the, the, the minds of these people, we discussed the house in detail and went through each room you know like . . . yes . . . like a team of forensic scientist looking for clues . . . we looked at this we looked at that a beautiful house mind with fantastic views across the Wettersham Valley it does have rolling hills and valleys but the cost was never mentioned. Struttclyde asked the pertinent question why we, Wooten & Struttclyde, were asked to attend the meeting as surly the sale or purchase is not a matter for our company. The gentleman whose name I cannot disclose for the purported confidentiality of deeds said in no uncertain terms that they require the earthly assistance of Wooten & Struttclyde and our warm and friendly human approach in these matters, well, of course we did not question the deeds but offered our experience'.

'I see' said Jack.

'Well for a fee of course' James admitted

'So is the house sold then'? Ask Jack.

James recoils in his chair and is angered by Jack and his reproach.

'Your question defies reason Jack' . . . . retorted James.

'James & Struttclyde have received good comments from a competitor and I can assure you that you will be better served if you stay well clear of that place' He offered his advice.

'Well thanks for the advice James I didn't mean to offend, but it is just that I have plans for that place, to . . . make a tidy fortune and birds do not talk.' Jack lent forward towards James as he replied. He was in no mood to take advice.

'I understand Jack but you also need to understand that I did not meet you here . . . ! (James looks at his watch part way through his sentence) . . . by chance, by the way what time is it? 'My watch seems to have stopped; oh dear!'

Jack takes a glance at his watch.

'Oh . . . it is 9:30am James'.

'Oh damn! I must go I have got to dash'. James picked up his cup to finish drinking his Americano.

'I will see you no doubt Jack; you always were one to make up your own mind'.

The sentiment was accepted by Jack but James wanted him to listen for once and take his advice.

'Make up your own mind then' James conceded

James offered a knowing wink to Jack before he raised his huge bulk off the leather clad chair he was sitting on then nodded a couple of times toward his friend, then said, I will see you later'.

It was as though, an act was done by one who knows the potential of the outcome and the advice he gave was good advice and the advice was as he wished that his friend would take but James had to accept the fact that Jack Law was set and intent, the deed was done by his word.

'I hope to see you again' was James's last word.

It is a half of an hour to go before his meeting with the stranger, that woman he had spoken with on the phone. Jack considered the events of the morning and was now feeling a lot better than he did the moment before he had had the chat with James, James Wooten whom for now was long gone.

'Hey Ruby . . . Thanks see you later'. Jack finishes his coffee and orange and gets up to leave Rubies coffee shop and heads out toward the street he left a couple of bills on the table.

He has an easy and serene feeling about him as he hears the light rail train overhead as he walks under the light rail bridge. It is but a short walk to his office from Rubies coffee shop it is an office which he shares with Delia. Delia could open up shop if he has not arrived she has a key and has the set codes for the intruder alarm system, she would collect mail and sort them if any mail was delivered for that matter and answer any phone calls take messages etc, etc . . . The walk allowed him to cover the remaining minutes before his meeting with the mysterious caller.

Jack arrives at his office and opens the office door but his entry alarms Delia just as she is about to sit down at her desk.

'Oh morning Jack how are you . . . you gave me a fright. Sorry but you startled me' she confesses. Nevertheless it was not her fault that Jack ploughed his way into the office space.

'I just put down the phone, the lady you spoke with is just around the corner says she is on time and will be here in a couple of minutes. She sounds really nice Jack who is she, did not leave a name or nothing'

Delia inquires of Jack for some response but he whom by now has said nothing.

'Good morning Delia' his reply was sarcastically retorted a hint that Delia was acting like a nosey parker, he pointed to his nose and taped it twice.

But he allowed her that one and was tapped his nose jokingly.

'Yes' he offered back, with a rather telling admission.

'She is a bit of a spook though'

Jack could only muster up the word spook to describe the woman he had nothing else.

'Hey! But forget that, any mail today Delia?'

'No . . . !. no mail today Jack, nothing'.

Jack walks up to his desk and picks up a manila envelope which is placed in full view for all to see.

'What's this then Delia?'

Jack looks at Delia waving the envelope in the air.

'Oh . . .' she paused . . . 'Oh; I don't know maybe you left it there yesterday I don't know Jack'.

'To hell I did!'

Delia looked at Jack and stopped what she was doing and removing herself from her own leviathan task, something Jack said really got her attention and he looked a picture of awe.

'Wow! You look like you have just seen a ghost' she said

Jack had become a sudden shade of pale grey and ashen like and looking at the clock it was exactly 10:00am. Delia got up and walked over to him and took the envelope from Jack as easy as taking sweetie from a baby . . .

(Have you ever tried taking sweetie from a baby?)

. . . and opened it.

Jack who was normally cool and nonchalant was sweating so he wiped what he could from his forehead using a thumb. He wanted to but didn't know how to explain his fear but he made an effort . . .

'Delia wait let me explain something' he went on to say, but as Jack was about to share his experiences of the morning with Delia she pulled out the contents and showed them to him.

'Jack look it is a letter from an estate agent called Spherewell Housing Ltd. she starts to read slowly and methodically.

'There is a picture of that house in Wettersham you know the one the one that you are interested in buying'

Delia continued to read the contents and relayed the details to Jack who was now overcome within himself and unable to make sense of all the events which were taking place he looked at the office door waiting for the woman to arrive. Yet the woman never came and yet there were no further calls from her.

Delia hadn't any idea of what is going through Jacks mind at that time or what he might be feeling, she hadn't listened to Jack when he tried to explain. But Jack, he knew . . . he realised though, the woman had kept her word and that she had come just like she said . . . She said 10:00am.

'Delia . . . !'

Jack prepared himself and took the contents from Delia just as easy as she had taken them from him. (Like taking sweetie from a baby)

'I'll take those let me have them give them to me Delia; I am going to have to check this out myself'

'Spooky Huh . . .' Delia teases him.

'You are one who has to make up your own mind are you not Jack?'

Delia uttered the very same words which James Wooten had uttered and those words echoed around and about his head, bouncing off the walls of his cranium.

'You are one who has to make up your own mind are you not Jack?'

'You are one who has to make up your own mind are you not Jack?'

'You are one who has to make up your own mind are you not Jack?'

Jack snatched the sheets of paper demanding and shouting at the top of his voice . . .

'Shut up! Please shut the hell up!! . . . STOP' and held his head

The envelope and some of the contents fell to the floor.

He had to get out of the office and maybe head back home but anywhere as long as it is away from Delia. With what he held on to he headed along the streets he had trod many times thinking home is the only place where he could think straight. The sound of the light rail thundered around him as he walked under the light rail bridge the wheels of a train screeched and thundered along the tracks, he passed Rubies coffee shop he noticed her looking out of the window at him, Ruby did not smile or wave she just looked at him her head never moved but her eyes followed him just like the portraits, her eyes followed him as he went by and people on the road stared at him even people who knew him not or so he thought but Jack carried on relentlessly back toward his home. Each step he took was as purposeful as the first. It is here that we see the first signs of man intent. A moment of rage came about his mind the atmosphere above had opened up to reveal the night sky, and, suddenly he stopped walking, he stirred to read from page one of the letter:

There is a small house located at the end of this path. It bares not a living occupant but all the local dwellers fear that this house holds the key to the whereabouts of the last child of Mrs. Ruanple.

A voice from behind Jack Law says. 'I dear you to enter in and see for yourself where there be a lost child dead in there'.

Jack turned on a sixpence!!

He saw not a soul but the way from hence he came but with trees and dead grass and leaves still falling around. Jack then turned back only to face a small house sited at the end of a path.

He had only a moment to gather his senses one second he is on a road in the city and the next a strange place in the middle of what seemed nowhere yet looking at the same small house and he himself standing there on this path. The very same path which takes you to that small house, this was the moment enough though for in that second Jack Law had to gather his senses.

A couple of leaves floated down in front of his face he reached out and caught one of them between his fingers the leaf was crisp and crumpled easily to a fine dust opening his hand he let it continue on down to the ground and catching sight of his right foot as he watched the crumpled leaf he noticed that the ground bore footprints and the placement of his right foot was fitted neatly into one of them. He stepped out of it quickly but as sure as day the footprints led up to the gate of the small house. The sun was at this time high in sky only a chill was in the air and like someone breathing on your neck you would swear that you were not alone. But Jack would not turn about again but he would gather two more steps closer to the small house. So, now as he got closer it would appear to him just how old the view from that first floor window could be and it occurred him also what it would be like, there is nothing worse than being in the constant reminder of the past he thought and how he himself might have been raised but something drew him yet nearer and unwittingly he put himself in that position.

It was the 15th birthday of a minor and the day a child institute celebrating his return to society his friends or carers and a couple of doctors in white overalls greeting him with goodbye farewells and the probation officer of the Governmental council who received him the rest was forgotten about. A file marked confidential was stamped with approval for release and sealed the file will be kept with other secret documents and locked away the only other entry on the cover of the file was the name Mrs Jaclyn Peldon.

Jack saw a youth standing at the window looking out but the youth was acting suspiciously he hid to the side but he could clearly see the youth was pumped up also his eyes were bulging then in full view he held up a pistol and blew his head off.

Was that real did that really happen, his imagination was vivid but a far cry from being in the middle of nowhere the shot rang out with a sickening thud a single shot but all Jack could do was to stay transfixed by the vision. The window become darkened and the youth was gone the sound of footsteps followed behind him he looked down and saw his shoes touch the earth. The shoes he saw were white with real Canadian tassels they were not clean yet worn down and fit his feet neatly the footprints are unmistaken, size 9, and Jack wears size 9 but those shoes were never his.

In an air of silence, no birds could be heard singing, no flapping of wings only the trees in their abundance as they swayed in the distance and around about an atmosphere in a second seemed like even less still but for no matter and for this reason only, that is, that time passes only in the mind.

'Have I been here before? But I don't know this place' Jack questions himself and mumbles like a half mad unstated lunatic.

'Well now you may wonder' a reply comes like a swirling wind.

He had taken one more step forward equal to the footprints already moulded into the earth and besides himself he turned about once more in panic but his torment shook a sparrow from its perch and its flapping slipped into the distance. He walked backwards but slowly a couple more steps still equal to those footprints moulded in the earth and the more he becomes perplexed and puzzlement adored his look like a cloak he turned about yet again to face the house for the house was the greater magnet and for Jack one more step was enough to keep him from the gate the burning desire for knowledge made Jack inquire.

'Who's there?' . . . He had to know this but he could not make demand of this knowledge as much as he wanted it but like beggars he must plead.

'Who is there . . . I beg of you make yourself know'. Jack changed his tone.

Fear had taken hold of his mind for he knew not the voice or from whence it came and yet no soul was to be found, even the path he stood upon seemed narrower now and enclosing it was as if the way out had changed and the only advantage was to go to or even past the little house. He felt the house heave, and knew, somehow he was under its gaze and even certain that he was being watched, something in the trees or maybe from the tawny windows, the bricks maybe. Jack tried to pull himself together and studied his watch when he noticed that the time was 09:48am and the little hand was going backwards by the second.

'Good morning' a young voice herded towards him, 'do not be afraid'.

Indeed, a young woman took his attention away from the peculiar motion of his time piece.

'My name is April'.

Surely spring was in her voice for she sounded like a flute with an angels harp for harmonics, he thought.

'You talk with song in your voice' . . .

'You add a new dimension to this day' . . .

'Bb . . . Bb . . . But where are you? You sound so young and melodious, are there more of you . . .' Jack stammered.

Suddenly he became almost muted, utter tremble was with him, he looked around . . . then his eyes fell upon . . .

'April . . . !'

To an onlooker it would have been a scene like a discovery, yet . . . unbeknownst to him he acted as if he had known April from somewhere, not as much a startle though for this much it was a surprise it was because he could not account how he knew the girl or whence from, and furthermore, she . . . April was standing by the gate just inside the front yard of the house. Jack shook his head in disbelief and thumbed an inquiry.

'How comes I did not see you before, I was merely one step away?' he asked.

'Trouble yourself not with this for I have something to show you'. She replied in a muddled form of English not heard for centuries.

April wore a frock, a white floral frock with a yellow ribbon tied at the back and subtle lace hem which hung below her knees and hovered above her shoes exposing her white socks and black shoes with buckles a neck line unusual the style and also not seen for many, many years, the frock had a distinct pattern of bouquets not dissimilar to a bridal bouquet and yes the frock fit April like a glove, she glowed in the early morning light. As Jack admired her she glowed brighter, brighter and brighter he was forced to squint and lose focus until he closed his eyes flashes continued to fill his retina.

The sun, now, was lower in the sky looking toward the east and still orange, still with his eyes closed Jack Law was stirred as if awakened from a dream, and he had found himself standing inside the front yard of the house not knowing how or when he had entered through the gate, raising his arm he went to stroke his brow with the wrist and remembered he had a problem with his watch it would be the same arm he wore the watch on. Jack moved his head to study his watch for the second time the hands of the watch now showing 08:02pm, he looked for April but April was gone the little hand was still travelling backward by the second.

Jack had never known fear like this before but the feeling he had made him real scared, he neither understood nor had any idea why he was being haunted by the ghost of a girl or how he ended up on this path does he go on try to find a way out, the fear of the unknown was made worse especially when time appears to be going backward and the sun being in the west in the morning and why was it fucking orange, none of it made sense, he knew going back was not an option he had to go forward, but even that made no sense either.

'Think! Think!' he tried hard to come up with an answer.

'Come on man think!' Jack started talking out aloud he was trying to talk himself out of the torment and the fear this nightmare had on him, he needed a way out.

"Ok . . . Ok. In a helpless position he decides to resign, 'less panic' he figures might help and considering his situation, 'maybe another check on the time' he thought out aloud, might help also. This was his only course of action and the only action out of the despair he could think of, so he figured that it was the time that was wrong and musters up the courage to adjust his watch and convinced he could put a stop to his troubles attempted to change it . . .

'Whoa . . . ! Hold on'

Jack felt himself being drawn along into the house he could see the front door opening there was nothing he could do to turn away from it his eyes filled with grief and the pain etched his grin. April was standing at the open door. His stance was that of a tug-o-war but the opposition's strength was overbearing he tried with all his might to free himself but could not.

'Come . . . Come . . . Come you BASTARD! Come see! Can you smell burning?' she emphasised with vile contempt for her captive.

April's voice was sounded out but had changed to disgusting rather than the sweet girl who greeted him at about 10:00am, her breath reeked of death and that sweet dress she wore was turned to dead flowers thrown together with hemp and straw. If he could only turn away from her vile passion but her pleasure grew and seeing that he could not resist the strain she'd put upon him, she tugged on the invisible rope pulling Jack toward the door, she was horrible and excited and grinning as she tugged and Jack with both feet had no foothold slid nearer and nearer as she tugged mocking him.

The heat inside the house was set with mould and clung to the air all about the house it was very humid and there was no light either but a glare created by the freakish sun, the sound of his Tokiax ri rang out but his arms were locked tight he could not answer it or see the display but it quickly dawned on him then that it was April calling.

'Hello is that you Jack?' he heard her voice coming from the phone.

In his panicked state he recalls the woman he had spoken to on the phone she promised to reveal her purpose to him at 10:00am but it was Delia that had opened the envelope revealing the documents regarding the purchase of the house. But still he had no idea why this sad excuse for a woman would be akin to him.

'What do you want from me? . . . Let me go! . . . . 'still he tries to fight back.

'We are not holding you' the sounds of two voices groan in the dark gut ridden renking room.

'We!? Who the hell is we, how did I get here . . . !? . . . Where am I?'

Jack demands answers to the unnatural fate he has found himself the fear has is coupled with anger feels he needs protecting so he pleads for help.

'Help yourself if you can'

'When you feel like it you do, do you not Jack?' the question was asked as part of an accusation but the English was wrong and outdated.

The voice of a man yields some truth out of the gloom but the unknown man mocked him and following his statement a sense of recollection and flashes of the past were there to remind him. It was a wretched fire that burnt orange against darkened room. The walls were stripped bare by the fire.

'Yes! He sees now . . .' the voice emits out of the null. 'And I Judge Demus will commit thee to death by fire if thee is found to be guilty'.

Jack could see into the filth of the darkness and senses that he had been there before, but for now he just wanted out of it.

'Let me out!'

'Let me out' Jack repeats.

'No not yet welcome back to your tent, did you forget your works? it is within death that the wicked will be taunted until memory returns' dulcet tones of Judge Demus Trause emit from the null.

Although not seen the judge bears down on the suspect and the darkness plays Jacks mind and for a while but the images of a fire flicker by with the putrid smell of burning skin creeping up his nostrils his clothes are set on fire he is burning up Jack tries to move towards his tormentors but he cannot see them Jack steps forwards onto nothing and suddenly is falling April is falling with him also, as the two fall together April grins with an ugly gape, her teeth were not that of any young woman taunting and mocking Jack she cries out.

'Yes . . . oh yes! You remember, the fall, will it kill you, it will kill anyone?'

The floor is damp and cold the sky is clear one could count every star in the night sky and there be an owl watching over its terrain the owl's song echoes through the cold night air.

Too Wit Too Wooo . . .

Too Wit Too Wooo . . .

Jack is stirred by the owls song and is awoken, the owl whom seems to be stirred also seems very interested by such an odd heap slumped on the ground how odd to the owl this must seem, the heap is so odd that it compels the owl to take flight and with one great swoop the great tawny sweeps close gliding right over Jacks head Jack had no escape but stirred not to move he cowered low to the damp earth where he lay then he thinks that he is still burning and frantically swats all about himself and jumps too his feet but there were no sign of fire or anything burnt. Jack fully recovers and stands himself upon the ground he sees the big tawny owl circling way in the distance above this small house and from what appears to be a path under the star lit sky Jack stood looking towards the house and peers at his watch he is is puzzled and struggles with intent as to how or why he is back again outside he searches his pockets but finds only his wallet and keys so instead he then looks at is watch again this time he notices the second hand is going backwards by the second.

'Damn, the darned thing must be busted'

He can neither remember how he escaped the fire the seconds before nor even the hours; for his predicament is this . . . . he does not remember the past but this is his future . . . . Or at least for Jack the predicament of the future will depend on his past and the past is catching up with him and with each second that comes his memory will return.

Rummaging through his pockets in an hap-hazard fashion not really knowing what he is looking for Jack Law takes another look at his watch it is now 03:12am a piece of paper on the ground by his foot takes his attention away from the coming seconds as they tick towards his past.

It reads . . .

Time passes my Love yet my Love passes me by . . . darling . . .

Jack has an unassuming confused look upon his face as the rest of the note is being torn away like the sand in an hourglass but the date was clear enough to read to down to the year

March 16ᵗʰ 172 . . .

'Seventeen hundred . . . seventeen hundred'

He repeats the date to himself again and again trying to recall something or memory, something out of the history books for that period that day that month, the sweat on his face thickens, the fear in him rises and his heart thumps louder as a mist moves low to the ground from betwixt the trees on his left and is then swallowed up by the trees on the opposite side. He makes a decision to gather pace but slowly towards the small house for cover down the path trying to ignore the thing his heart beating faster than each step, his steps quicken as approaching from behind the sound of laughter and revelry is coming toward him, urged to turn around to face the onslaught two men and a woman rushed past causing Jack to spin he is spun a quarter turn then suddenly finds himself rotating at the same pace as the gaiety that had breezed past, the trees, bushes, sky, earth, everything in his sight turns to a blur as he is spun round and round and round, sweeping him off his feet, and then images of fire, again he himself is alight as he is spun round and round.

'Maybe this fire is your doing, something to do with you maybe'

A sarcastic accusation is reeled off as the spinning continues, he hears the charge clearly but knows not where it came from and yet in his vision Jack sees an young girl falling . . . holding hands with a young man and both appear to be in pain and screaming as they fall then he sees them burnt up and he himself is burnt to sinters. The accusation was meant as a hint, it seems there is a time line that must not be reached, the human mind cannot remain in this realm the and fellows were becoming impatient.

'It is time to raise the woman that wandered into our realm, Charlise. The Higher Decree has revealed a common attitude between you and the poor soul her strength has waned since you went out to join the séance. When I give order for the agreement to be heard it was fondled but you hid the truth did you not'

'That is contempt' says Carlos

'Is this the reason you feared he die' Timothy was staring at Shelia as he asked his first question of her.

'I bid you fellows to let the revelation come from the mind he has it and he will reveal what happened and why this soul trespassed into our realm'

The Judge Demus Trause spoke the trail and immediately the fellows clasp hands and looked toward the stars but whilst doing so Shelia made a quick glance back at Carlos. She already knew that her cat was out the bag.

Meanwhile . . .

'Jack . . . Jack wake up . . . ! Wake up Jack. You cannot sleep here you know, you must stay awake'.

Finally his slumber is broken and he awakes and finds himself lying down on the cold ground.

'Jack Law I feared you had gone away again'

After the apparent experience with vision and revelation he passed out and fell to the ground where he stood but lying on his back.

'Who are you calling Jack my name is not Jack and I don't know of any Law either?' he finds himself looking up at a blurred image stooped above him barely able to open up his eyes, he sneezed loudly causing the flashes reappear.

'You must not worry, please do not trouble yourself, but you can't stay here, come, come with me to my house, come on it is more comfortable and warm'.

He uses his hands to feel around him as if to secure himself as he gingerly opens one eye the other he hardly opens as he scans around and about, then he rises up from off his back and sits upright as a woman helps him to his feet she would accompany him to the house and take him inside and he would follow her upstairs to a bedroom.

'You can sleep here if you like it is up to you' she says.

He really didn't have an option though, but to take the woman's offer, the strength to resist was not there either it was easier to follow, however, so he followed. Upstairs his eyes became use to the surroundings, the light in the room created by a lantern placed curiously on the sideboard an antique looking piece over on the other side of the room. It was not long before he fell asleep having sat on her bed.

Jack Law . . . Mr Law . . . Jack wake up . . . Hey wake up Jack. You cannot sleep here you know you must stay awake, it was a woman's finger gently jabbing at his side but this time it was meant to wake him up.

'Who's sleeping . . . ? Who's fooling around with me . . . Who the hell are you . . . ?"

Jack makes to his feet as if commanded by an army officer, only this time it is the fear of the unknown that controls him, his stance is upright as if beckoned by a general, yet no, he is frightened, frightened out of his life and it is this fear which makes him stand but it is his mind which is brought to attention, attention brought on by a silken voice of an adult, an adult woman one could tell had knowledge and patience much like a private courtesan a high class woman a dedicated housewife even a mistress.

"You do not remember me do you . . . ? Let me remind you".

From behind the lantern he had made out the image of the woman, but how can this woman just appear from nowhere, the woman and the lantern somehow manoeuvres towards him but the light from lantern creates a ghastly looking person behind it and a strong scent of kerosene fills his nostrils, Jack is overcome by the fumes and can barely see the woman's face blinking his eyes earnestly for he is just as anxious to know who the woman is, this ghostly apparition that becomes more real the closer and closer it comes, fear did not matter the woman certainly had Jacks attention. It was all-a-sudden then when the ghostly apparition becomes what is definitely a woman, the woman holding the lantern is a beauty, maybe eastern or south American for her skin was like olive and soft looking her hair very long and full, her eyes dark and full of want, this made her locks seem even alive and deep auburn in colour, she would make a portrait that many a man would admire, and her lips had moisture, ready to kiss, more red, so giving easy a focal point to succumb or surrender to, was it her seduction had she tried that made Jack forget the torment so close so introvert that Jack tasted the nerve of temptation even in a place like this or the fact he was in no state resist. This woman had to be real Jack felt. Her stare was not ready and passion gave way to enquiry and reality that he had power to only inquire with gusto.

'What do you want from me . . . how did I get here?' ask Jack "Where am I" Jack demands answers to the many questions he fires off.

"So many questions Jack, do not anger yourself for I am slow to anger myself and you know what they say, beware of a woman scorned so calm yourself my darling".

Her motion towards Jack is deliberate and giving Jack Law enough time to search her intention and each movement was for him to obtain himself.

'Woman scorned! What do you mean a woman scorned?' he asks

She moves up towards him cat like as if he were prey her eyes now proper in his view, he can now see who the is . . . and she the woman reveals herself.

The dull light in the room was insignificant; the full impact of the lantern has played its part.

Mrs Ruanple, he said, assuring that he knew her. Jack could not hide the disbelief when he revealed of the many years that this woman who has not been seen by anyone and the years he himself had searched, for many years he emphasised, over his own dead body the love of his life was standing before him as real as the morning.

'But what is this?!' I feared you dead it just cannot be, I . . .'

Before he could utter another word Mrs Ruanple took hold of Jacks left arm and raising it so that he caught sight of the time piece he wears.

'Do you know what time it is, do you even know the date, I see you remember a name clearly do you remember this room?'

'Do you even know where you are Mr . . . ?'

Mrs Ruanple took the stance as if ready to pounce on her catch.

'Do you remember what you did?'

That final question came like blow from a dagger.

Jack retreated and sat back down on the bed, he studied his watch like a boy who had just been taught a lesson . . . 7:45pm and the second hand still going backwards by second. Mrs Ruanple let go of his left arm her feelings now satisfied knowing she has brought some message across to him.

Mrs Ruanple acted the woman who must always get her way, she was very forceful and her woman was just so, woe to the lucky man lucky enough to attract her charm.

The answers to his many questions were finally being answered but it is he who has the answers to them, and realising that he has gone backward in time and that he has, somehow, gone back several years from the day he remembers vividly the visit to the Grey Lawn. He remembers standing by the graveside which bears no name and which is to be, actually, many years later. It was the date on that piece of paper that he pulled from his pocket that called the measure, 1720. He stood up from the bed and paced around, it puzzled him to think that he had had it appears, had had some sort of business with that person buried in an unmarked grave, and with Mrs Ruanple also, but it puzzled him more as to why he became puzzled to realise that fact. The confusion triggers more revelations.

'He is going awaken' fears Timothy.

'If he does then let it be, The Higher Decree would have determined it. Please keep your hands clasped' Judge Demus Trause remains confident.

Shelia Charlise says nothing.

Jack Law, recalls the a day when all this began that day he had set off to view, as it is written, a modest desirable residence in idyllic settings near woodlands off kettling Village boasting good views across the Wettersham valley and accessed by a path worn together by the locals and ramblers and walkers, and said to be well sought after. He has the recollection and says . . .

'June . . . ?'

'That's right, nobody calls me June but you Jack, nobody'.

Mrs Ruanple, her real name was Grace, she was a real beautiful woman whose curves fit the very parts of her woman and she still looks every part as homely as she moves around the room she stands at the window and looks out across the valley and Jack moves back and stands by the edge of the bed and rest a hand on the headboard he admires the descent figure in his sight his thoughts drift toward her his soul traverses about her, he imagines exactly what Grace Ruanple sees out from that window and imagines himself standing next to her, he had seen the view many times before. Wettersham Valley was at its best when viewed from that first floor window the sun going down gave the trees distinction a boast of colour the full broad spectrum areas of land carpeted with fallen leaves yellow, brown and grass green, the patience of the woman was intense as she waited for Jack still, she waited till voices like song, and, his voice was at her ears like a whisper, the crisp tingle of cymbals like breath, the conductor instructs his orchestra to play the strings of their harps, time and time again he visited her after that day, and the memory now repeats itself. He wraps his arms about her waist and June was still for him so that he could feel the woman in her, not for the view from the window as much as the touch that was given up like wind soft and comfortable with its strength it sends the willing to go through the act time and time again and again. It was enough to turn her about to detail the forge between them, the moisture on her lips the want of her lire sealed it, her eyes grew darker and the glaze was ready hesitation had no place here. He mounted his June there by the window as she bent forward it was so easy the way her frock was raised to reveal even greater the thighs that would part, the passion that was found in her kiss, would surely slain the afflicted, but her mouth had not guilt but want, and June wanted him. They made love right there by the view overlooking the valley from that window.

It is so forbidden for a married woman to have behaved like that, there was an era when many would frown upon her, even turn away from her in shame and a manner that would make even the most hardened of co-habited minded relaters feel dishonour, but when want churns the feelings for love and wanton behaviour beckons the heart who on earth could put question or restraint on those feelings or to be evermore real, prohibit, to resist temptation, who has never felt overcome with the temptation insomuch that they walk away from temptation itself, certainly though, in his case temptation was his mentor, he was there for the remit, he was there not to resist, he was there to commit the sin and she the willing wife was there as the tempestuous most provocative of woman she wore Sophia as her undergarments for him only.

The thoughts continued to haunt the loins of his mind after the act, but this was untypical of him, normally he would not feel guilty and move on to the next conquest that maybe so but he could not resist her, there was an inimitable passion, he felt it as he and Grace made love, differing from any other time or lover, she touched his soul this time and when he came off and down from his mount he finds himself looking at his watch again, the time is 6:15pm and satisfied he meandered in backward motion macho-like having pulled his trousers up leaving the them unzipped to lounge on the bed.

'My lover this was our last time, then it happened'

'What do you mean, what are you talking about . . . what do you mean by then it happened?' the mood was more relaxed now and he would have preferred to go back to sleep with his June next to him.

Grace spoke softly to him the sound of her voice had taken his mind away from his troubles and he found himself looking at her fine curves exposed but only briefly she pulled her frock, it slowly slipped down to cover her body.

'Your husband's a lucky man' he says.

The involuntary admission is offered as Jack Law continues to admire her as she remains over by the window to admiring the views of the Wettersham Valley.

'June . . . Grace . . .' Mrs Ruanple' calling out the many names 'my husband will be home soon' she says but he continues to watch and admire the woman as she stands and stares out the window, waiting for her next word.

'Do you even know where you are?' she mocked him.

'I' do not . . . but with you June everything feels just fine, but as you ask, something isn't quite right' he admits whist rubbed his eyes.

He was about to ask her what was going to happen if her husband knew of their affair and lifts his head towards where June was standing but she is not there, she has gone, disappeared.

'How dare you . . . turn around . . . !' the sound of a strong man's voice hissed in tongue is heard from behind the wall behind Jacks head and a pounding on the front door downstairs he hears it loud and clear the hell has returned.

'Turn around' a voice full of the sound of hiss much like the sound a snake again the voice demands of Jack in a weird whisper that caused the window curtain to flap. Jack is frightened out of his skin his eyes seem to pop out and his eyebrows knit together, but, dare Jack turn around to face his tormentor, not this time the pounding on the door was even more menacing Jack feared he would be in a greater danger if the, what sounded like a monster poundings at the door came in.

'My God!' he lets out a scream as a sense of urgency surmounts him.

'I need to leave this place, to all the hell of my years this woman haunts me and I am here why me what have I done I must wake up'.

The room in which the woman gave Jack rectitude is different now but the woman has gone the lantern is placed on the sideboard just as it was, but it is darker now with not much light and the day is not the same either it is raining outside the woman and her presents seems long gone but the lantern still burns but achieving only a dim light. Jack Law reaches out and grabs the lantern and with a swift move he turns to smash the fiend behind him, the picture he makes is that of a man full of fear holding the lantern in one hand and the other a clenched fist his face etched with pain with teeth snarled like a dog, he spun a half turn a quarter turn right and back again there was nothing even no one there but himself, Jack was the only fiend in the room a man completely out of his mind. The pounding on the door stopped and the dim light created by the lantern it seems to wane then extinguish, now, Jack is in the room alone in darkness his heart rate has shot up and is clearly visible as it beats in his chest and can be heard above the silence in the room therein. Jack remains still but observes the blue of night at the window then Jack turns his head towards the hand which holds the lantern his body makes an involuntary shiver the piece of antiquity disappoints him so he throws the useless lantern into the darkened room. A huge flash of light lifts up from where the grand glass moulded specimen lands Jack sights three people in the flash but they are burning up and screaming, they scream as the fire takes hold of them they burn and scream out in great pain the pounding at the door starts again the whole house buckles to the monster and the sound of voices and echoes walk along the walls like ripples across water, the three people in the fantastic fire burn as fire grips the skin they scream louder and louder Jack turns away from the sight and the shrilling cries so horrific they burn at his ears till his hair catches alight this causes him to murmur a low cry of atonement realising he himself is in danger of now burning up he launches himself at the window and jumps forth to save his own his life and away from the scorching furnace he created.

'There be a small house at the end of this path just follow your nose you cannot miss it'

An instruction is volunteered by an older looking man with a straw held between his teeth.

'That'll be right now, 'tis a beautiful house too mind'

'Belongs to Mrs Ruanple' offers an elderly lady.

'Her husband be missing, some say he be gone away with another woman, that's silly, I know he be dead alright, they had a child you know, she was born in the month of April, yes, she was a darling child, very beautiful, she grew up nice and become a kind and generous child not to be mistaken mind, no what I mean . . . she was very playful, not really sure where she got her name though, April, tis a nickname maybe, much like June, a nickname, she be gone to . . . missing. They are all missing!' said the old lady.

The last statement spoken by the old woman jabbed like a dagger and was meant to instil some thought provoking link to which she may hope would bring fourth truth from the visitor.

'There be secrets that will never be kept secret, time will tell on you'

He heard more voices and they were scratching at his ears and irritating his nerves the relentless tirade of information and the barracking taunts thrown around betwixt these unknown volunteers that had gathered around the unsuspecting visitor the babble sounded like they were deliberating but Jack Law suffered to be in that place at that time. Having just escaped what can only be described as a ferocious inferno only to be standing yet again on this path in the valley called Wettersham with no sign of a fire at all he was amazed and relieved that he himself was not hurt or burnt when he had leapt from the window. Jack Law gave sudden attention to the onlookers, there was no fire at all but he quickly realised that these people were gathered for his sake only, and his mind had more revelations for him to reveal.

A young girl was there also in the crowd she had a might strange look on her face as she repeated what the old woman had said.

'They had a child to you know' pointing straight at the elderly lady.

'Yes yes' says the old woman. 'Did you not know that? She was young and innocent only sixteen.' . . . pointing her finger at him.

'Now now you two lets try to be nice for the stranger he can never guess this but we be around here many days now' the older looking man takes charge. 'Many people come and go'

'Yes yes' repeats the elderly lady. Seems her vocabulary is limited.

'But none stay' the older looking man continues. 'Not unlike you sir'

'Yes yes, you have come a long way, haven't you Jack Law?'

He shudders at the mention of his name but has no time to utter a word as the sally continues with their advance.

'You insisted that she put it on the market, the house that is'. The old man says.

'Yes yes'. The elderly woman's repeated acknowledgement of the facts were becoming evermore distressing, she even sounded like a battling barrister standing in a courtroom

'Yes the very fact is true, sir'

'Indeed an ingenious plot to attract a buyer or maybe just your way of hiding something?' asked the old woman, badgering the fellowman. 'Yes, let's put it on the market'

The old woman was very annoying her voice etching at his skin, he could tell the old woman had more than just neighbourly thoughts in her heart but for now all he could do was listen as he scratched an annoying itch on his upper arm.

The young girl studies Jacks shoes then begins to look him up slowly from the corner of her eyes then fixed a smug stare into his. Jack stared back at her like a rabbit caught between the headlamps of oncoming car or something even more alarming, he was drawn into the girls staring eyes and trance like he could not blink even if he wanted to, the girls eyes told a story but he stood mesmerised by them . . . her eyes (that is) he wanted too but could not read or understand how the mystery being revealed to him was happening, but he saw a vision in the young girls eyes for sure, it was a picture of a young girl but it was the same young girl that was stood before him and in the background was the very house that rest on the end the path with a signpost clearly erected in the front yard, upon it was written . . . **FOR SALE** . . . and immediately appeared slapped diagonally across it came another sign so he could see . . . **SOLD** . . . !, in large red font

Jacks head jerked backwards like he had just been slapped on his forehead, Jacks fixation quickly disappeared.

'Can you see the house . . . you see the window? The young girl asked.

'My mother loved the view from there you know Jack Law do you not remember it yourself, you stand there like a frightened rabbit man, why do you come back now Jack? Can you not see for yourself?' although she was a young girl she was very forward in her reproach.

'It was I who had to make you return' revealed the older looking man.

'Perhaps you would like to go inside with us and see for yourself where there be inside the answers to the questions and suggestions about the missing souls and the mysteries and the goings on, you can tell us about it in there' the old man sounded persuasive, indeed the fickle will spell when enchanted.

Jack was held to the meaning and why the suggestions were being past at him but even more puzzled that these people even knew his name.

'Look . . .' he finally had the leeway to get a word in.

'Look, I don't know what is going on here or how on earth you all think you know me but my name is not . . . . not' he stumbled . . . or who you people are, and . . . and for gods' sake, how I even got in to this nightmare . . .' he came to a sudden halt and stopped his rant.

'That'll be alright now' said the older man, with a voice which would calm even the most ferocious of devils dogs or demons chasing down a petrified bunny rabbit.

'Yes yes' the elderly woman said with an increasing ridiculous greed that churned from her mouth.

'We be the locals . . . don't you see Jack, and we have been around here for the longest time awaiting, and awaiting for your return Jack'.

There were no needs for him to try and escape for that will had left him long ago and besides where could he run to, the little house of tricks . . . maybe back along the path to hence he came, no . . . ! None of these were options that would appeal, He knew the older man had the upper hand in this mystery and since people around here can appear and disappear he thought he would resign and wager it out.

'Look to hell with this nonsense, just tell me what is it that you all want to hear from me?' Jack Law demanded.

'No you look', said the older man 'look then at your time piece, that thing which you use to measure time, that thing you judge on your wrist look at it sir' the older mans tone rounded much smoother now and had a lure of contempt rather like setting bait with sweets, cheese would melt faster. The older man tempted jack. He surrounded Jack with an act that would impress a presiding judge ready to pass sentence over a suspect charged with a heinous crime.

'Yes yes, look at it . . .' needless to say the elderly woman had dribble on her lips she knew the truth was about to be revealed. Jack hadn't noticed until now that the young girl still had her eyes trained hard at him her eyebrows were positioned she insisted that he looked. She was very attractive but the look she wore had disapproval written all over it and that length of straw that the older man had between his teeth pointed toward Jack like a hammer when wielded by an adjudicator for order in court, the straw flicked up and down, up and down. It wasn't a smirk on the older mans face that worried Jack but the way that the old man's left eye squinted and his eyebrow moved upward, wink, wink . . . know-what-I-mean. He remembered Sir Brent Fuller his eyebrows were ff'd up too.

The talking ceased for a while giving Jack Law time to reflect but not for the first time he dared not look or take up any more offers for fear that he may just commit himself or find himself going backward further in time to face a fate more dread than the last.

'Ah . . . Jack . . . I note . . . you do not look at your contraption.' The older man pauses in between each conjuncture and behaves like a prosecutor, then continues.

The older mans index finger and knuckle nudges at the air around it. To Jack it sounded like someone knocking on a window pane.

Jack looks around to get some sense of his surroundings the air is warm and dry the sun sits behind a huge ominous cloud but still there is enough light blue sky and the trees show off the splendour of the many shades of green that they bear. It is indeed a nice day and for one to be on the path looking down toward the gate the gate that leads up to the door of the house and to be shrouded by such lush greenery and to be in such a place is a blessing such colour one should be satisfied with life but fate has cast an air of omen and not all seems quite like what it is. Jack looks at his accusers one by one from the older man to the young girl then the elderly woman and thinks to himself.

'Is this some kind of a kangaroo court? You people are not real even this place is not real. It's all fantasy I tell you . . . déjà vu'

As Jack ponders his merit he drifts off into a sort of daydream and speaks it out loud he is again woken to the reality that does haunt him.

'Déjà Vu you say that is interesting'

'We take note of what you have revealed in mind but the word must be uttered it is truth we seek' a voice unfamiliar he hears whispering to him.

'It could be déjà vu' Jack says to himself. 'But I feel like I know this place I have been here before'. He angles his head to get some measure of time, then to his watch, he was just about to check the time but again Jack Law is interrupted.

'Hello Jack . . . Jack wake up it's me darling come on we do not have much time'

April had grown into a teenager and wanted to explore the world, she wanted more the valley was beautiful, a real nice place to grow and to spend childhood but it was her age that changed, the days of exploring the green fields and streams, the streams which led to rivers and rivers which led her to dreams. Exploring wild life and birds, and insects . . . insects was never her thing though . . . she stared to explore her mother's things and even to ape her mother to the point of ape. Mother, was the next best thing to learn about. The girl she'd become watched her mother closely she even spied on her mother through hours of idle time and even through a hole in the garden fence shrouded by shrubbery and unbeknownst to her mother she watched her mother, she watched her mother and another man cuddle a man that was not her father, yet mother was happy to while away the minutes with a stranger even when father was away labouring, the man her mother knew and of whom she had told her daughter so little about, that she thought was just innocent, but not that day, that fateful day the innocent cuddle was lent to be idle and reckless, she saw that mockery was about her mother and he, he would act the willing player. An only child nearly spoilt but not neglected. Her youth taught her and the many hours of childhood play beguiled her, the real feeling of innocence made her the kind and generous girl that she became but in the stranger she saw betrayal she saw it in his eye as she peeped through the hole in the garden fence. It was a shock to her at first but she would not tell she did not want her father to know what was going on she did not want him to leave home for good or for her mother to leave either she kept that knowledge a secret to herself and told nobody. Over the course of time her innocents gave way and she became callous the secret that she kept to herself made her devious she learnt how to tell lies and she became conniving. It occurred to her that if she could come between her mother and her mother's lover that it would end the affair and developed a cunning plan. She teased Jack with her young woman even though she was girl she still had form and aped the frivolous ways of her mother to perfection yet quite playfully using her youth slowly she gains the attention of the man. In the valley outside the sun shone its light splendidly mother was away from the house, she had gone out and needless to say father was away too and not expected to return home for seven days April took the opportunity to arrange for her mother's lover to check by the house but making him believe that it was his lover that arranged a date she sent a letter to him written by hand and signed she had also learnt how to write just like her mother and signed it.

The Letter

To my darling Charles, I hope when this letter reaches you it finds you well, I am missing you too much to bear. Every day that passes I yearn more and more for your love. There is good news my love, John will be away for seven days. I hope you will come and stay close to me. Charles my bed is welcome to you my darling.

Monday week 12th August I have made arrangement for April.

Grace Ruanple . . .
                    .signed

PS . . . I Love you

The letter was written and sent to his home address.

It was a cunning plan April had cooked up but she could not have known that Charles had his mail redirected to his office in the city and the lady that shared his office space Delia would open up his letters anyhow, because these days people mainly receive business letters or just junk mail, but this one was hot and she read it the letter was real hot but she was not surprised as she knew he was an amorous and ardent lover but her time with him was over and out of spite she typed up a letter of her own she could have just discarded the love letter but she didn't she kept it, now her version was more businesslike she typed it in such a way that he would not clock-on to the that she had become party to his affair with the owner of that little house at the end of this path. She wrote . . .

The Letter

```
Dear Mr Charles Johnson'


Since you have shown a liking for my property.
I would like to take this opportunity and
invite you over to discuss the purchase.
If you are available, please come on Monday
week the 12ᵗʰ August.


Yours Faithfully
Grace Ruanple


Signed . . . .
```

The letter was typed.

Delia was satisfied with wording and its subtle tones. Using a scanning device she was able to lift the forged signature and transfer it onto the typed up letter and she and left it in Charles in-tray with all his other letters. But she was not finished.

The morning of the 12ᵗʰ Delia followed up her spiteful reaction to the original love letter and knowing that Charles always drank coffee she dosed his with a strong aphrodisiac tonic. It was a typical morning and she watched him drink it.

'This coffee taste different, but its nice Delia' he says

'Hmm that's good I am glad you like it have some more' Delia played a prank on her unsuspecting old flame. She was a little jealous that he was going on a date, a hot date with who she thought was Mrs Ruanple and Charles for that matter thought Delia was unaware of his love affair with Grace, the woman he calls June and for one whole week he allowed his thoughts to focus on the hidden subtlety at the mere mention of her property, he read it as it was meant to be read. He drank two whole cup full's of the concoction Delia had made that morning.

'Delia . . . I am out of the office all day. I will see you later' Charles got up to head off to his appointment.

'Ok . . . . Charles, I will see you later . . . (You dirty bastard!) She joked; but the last bit was said quietly under her breath so that he didn't hear it.

Charles arrives at the house but was disappointed to meet with April as she opened the door.

'Hello April how are you is your mother home' Charles acts polite but he was feeling quite rude.

'Hello Mr Charles, I am so glad to see you. My mother has gone out but she will be back soon, she said she is expecting you and ask me to let you in when you arrive'

'Oh' says Charles 'I think I'll better wait outside its not proper for me to be in the house alone with you. I'll just sit in my car' the aphrodisiac was working on him. Charles feels the effect and is almost turned on by April.

'You really look like your mother today . . . your hair . . . you're . . .' Charles paused, he spoke softly to April then turned to walk away but April followed him she remained cheerful and childlike'

'Mr Charles you don't have to do that mum said you can wait inside'

Aprils plan was failing she wanted Charles to enter the house to be alone with her, her plan was to lure Charles into a trap, as she had it her mother would arrive home and find Charles with her and she's struggling to get away from him screaming.

So she followed Charles as he walked and playfully takes his arms and lifts them up toward the sky, immediately he admires her firm breast, April was unaware that Charles was high, with ease and little effort he becomes like a trusting child himself and like a child April would play, Charles knew he had become aroused by her maturing body so feminine and alluring and her play suggested more to him than normal and for this he would let his feelings go, she just wanted to get him in the house , yet knowing the woman's daughter and the guilt, this did little now, the concoction Delia made was strong.

Now that the mind and the man would touch the frame with this light, things would get burnt. It was more than imagination for Jack Law when his lips felt the cold yet moist on her lips which tingled and would warm the spirit, arms were no longer in the air but cuddled around her body in a hold that appeared to grip. April kissed back but moved away her lips so that Charles could see them pout as the glint would feed for another taste. It was just as easy for April to pull away from his grip. April was full of life and fun loving and happy to feel the want that he had pent up for her she teased him as she ran toward the house she giggled like a menace he could only follow he was guided by the intense nature of her youth was he going to know her she makes his heart race his heart raced as he saw her run like a drugged giddy heroine turned on by her he reached out to catch her around the waist and spun her around to him it was her mouth he wanted. He was more aggressive now and with her he became more aggressive he played like a an amorous devil and pressed for an enormous taste of her moisture and a feel of her young breast her nipples now pointed and embossed against the limp material garment that she wore like only a woman can. April aped her mother to perfection. As the strap fell from her shoulder he would lick the skin about her neck it would have been impossible for April to leave now for she was rapped up in his spirit and as she gasped for one more breath Jack would smother her mouth for yet more of her soft and moist lips. The game fell to the ground amongst the green grass whilst the way to the house now out of mind. Was this what April had in mind for herself an older man old enough to be her father tearing away at her very life for every gasp of air she tried to gather Charles was there eating away at her body yet for her she clung to her task but gave up her woman for the feeling Charles had was brought on by an aphrodisiac tonic but he met his match in her and took April to the edge his hand reached up between her legs and with his fingers he touched her. April's mouth closed not even once but became so much more filled with want as she gasped Charles was busy between her legs finding the lace of her knickers, the amorous play the theatre the tune of foreplay was turning April on and on It must have been her last gasp or something when she gave up a groan . . . oh take me please take me he hesitated not and pressed his lips upon Aprils reddened mouth and smoothed her lips open as their tongues were found they hungered for and ate the passion and like a phenomenon a beast he was ready and entered her wetted pussy it was there he knew her and the fucked each other grinding their souls together on the ground April gasping was for air and he was riding his beauty for now she was even more appealing gave up the and he rode like Satan. His was possessed by June Ruanple and tonic was in him, but for her she was surly taken. Her hem stayed raised against her leg revealing her sweaty thighs as Charles thrust his intention deep into her woman continuously. Mother never came home.

In the heat of the moment he became aware that April had become still and her mouth still juicy but her stare was but a glaze yet she was not moving . . .

'April . . . April . . . !.Oh no Oh no, no, no.! My god! He sobers up quickly.

'Jack is it that you? Come back'

'Jack. You remember don't you Jack' the older man raises his voice.

'Oh no . . . Jack hears himself repeating the words as his focus on the old man standing a few feet away becomes clearer.

'Why are you sweating? He asks

Jack feels for his brow and realises that it is sweat and rubs his fingers together'.

'It was an accident I tell you it was never meant for her to die I don't know what came over me, we were making love I know it, I know it was wrong . . . so wrong but . . . the more wrong made for it to be more engrossing . . . the temptation, even the thought became a reality it was an accident, I don't know what was in me that day, it was so bad a terrible storm was brewing . . . a storm . . . a storm . . . I . . . I remember . . .'

Jack Law started to repeat himself and paused as he admitted to being there'

'What? is there can you tell me, can you tell me more' that voice he heard that unfamiliar whispering again.

Jack stood still looking towards the old man then he looked at the old woman with a certain sorrowful disdain, and the moment he looked at the old woman the wind picked up and started blowing stronger and stronger the locals that stood there fled as a man came running up a verge warning the coming of 'It' . . .

'It's coming run, run for your souls save your souls!' he shouted.

Just then an uprooted tree stump glided over his head he could see more people, people were running in the same direction but trying to get out of the way of the debris, likened to having a life of their own, the tree stumps flew like wingless birds, straight, they fall crashing to the ground releasing their weight and energy amongst the shrubbery on the earth an awesome sight to witness, he saw them in his vision and he heard their impact, they stood together the old man and old woman and the girl they watched as more uprooted trees and stumps and debris flung up into the air they seem to glide as if under control, the terrific wind had caused a bright blue sky to fade to a awesome grey, a vision of hell was seen, a tempestuous storm was at hand, Jack saw a tree stump hit a man slam on the back of his head there was a sickening thud the man had no chance, the storm blew hard against Jack's stance he and the old man and the old woman and young girl stood and watched the embracing horror, bracing only themselves against the strength of the phenomena, the phenomenon which gave rise to terror and fear, panic to the locals, yet, just as it started in an instant suddenly it stopped, the wind died down there were no more flying debris or uprooted trees gusting along, just a silent but eerie calm had returned to the valley, the sky gradually resumed its shade of blue, the trees in the distant seemed angry but swayed ever so lightly bowing to its strength, it was untenable yet it could come again.

'It was wild, really wild' . . . the thought of the storm coming again had triggered Jack into a narration of facts, he sneezed again he can see the flashes again but he seemed to be in definite knowledge of the facts. Jack stood still with the old people and young girl and related the facts to them.

. . . 'I had to do something I panicked but I could not flee the scene, she laid there still, not moving, dead I tell you . . . a storm came up from nowhere I had to think quick, my mind was still rude, it was then that I brought her dead body into the house but by the time I got to the house rain had soaked me right through and she, even her garments were soaked revealing that what had tempted me, I put her body down upstairs on the floor by the bed in that room see that window'

Jack pointed to the window the very window which he himself had flung himself from. The window which tells of the horrors and the pleasantries of an era and maybe even hides the torment of the crimes enacted over and over again.

'Then can you tell me more' the whispering voice asked of him to reveal more.

'Wait, be patient' Charlise 'Tis now he is in danger of awakening'

In turn and in a trance-like state he turned also his face towards the young girl then the old man but none of them were the person who whispers to him, he turns to the old woman but she only gives him a cold stare with what appeared to be a wizened apparel, his revelations were more than the old woman expected, she, was not the one either that whispered to him because the voice he hears was that of a woman that was not unfamiliar to him.

'What am I talking about I swear I . . . I!'.

Before Jack could utter another word from out of the colour and the surrounding trees the sound of voices could be heard.

'He knows what he has done . . . it's time to make him pay for his deed'

The voices are heard coming from the trees on his left.

'We've all seen him come and go'

'I'll be a witness . . . I'm a witness . . . I've seen him' tenders were heard all about, and on cue like the chorus in a hymn sung by a choir.

'Own up!' cried out the young girl 'Where be, the lost child'

'Quiet! All of you' the man's voice rocked 'I will have you all in contemp''

'It is time' he said 'look at the contraption you wear if you dear' the old man tempted him.

'Yes yes' the old woman danced with her song and poured guilt into his chalice. His heart started racing, the crazy people whom he did not know they surely knew of him, and, they test him as if they were his judge and jury.

'Look at your timepiece and tell us the rest' ordered the old woman.

Dread overcame him, he held back and refused the order, he was standing on path and looked towards the house and up to the very window he had just pointed to, he was about to flee the scene but like metal to a magnet he was lifted up off his feet he, the girl and old man were sent propelled towards the house he struggled against the force that lifted him but only to find himself again in the arms of April on the one side but with John Ruanple on the other.

'Hold him Father, hold him . . . !' she shouted. 'He is about to confess, he will reveal the truth from this subconscious mind and he will reveal it to us let the Judge Demus Trause hear the deed that was committed by the will of the Billet Society, the Society is survived by this mind and our memory lives in him'

She tried to stifle a giggle, but the level of April's charge against Jack Law was not so innocent, she had enticed Charles to be there that day, it was devious. Her plot was to gain her own satisfaction albeit and innocent cause, it was a deceitful act that would have led to—well—an innocent man being accused of a sexual assault.

The Billet Society holds no favour for those who are deceitful to a fellow therefore for and for this purpose only a charge has been heard and it goes against the deceitful plotter. So it shall be done.

'The cloak of deceit is made of hemp and straw, it will rub against the skin forever, tis true child that you spied afar your mother through a hole in the fence shrouded by shrubbery, yhea, and you rubbed up yourself for him thus did you derive at that course of action, that plot, and so that for yourself that you are not deceived also and by decree . . . Do not believe ye that the society be dumbed, that subconscious mind which we have hijacked no-eth it, thus we all know too, the inequity of youth befell you'

Yet again but for the finale to this conundrum the guilty fled, John and his daughter were slammed up against the wall of the house and the spirit of Jack Law entered through the very window he had bolted yet April was refused and John went.

It must have been hours that past since falling asleep, he thought, and indeed it couldn't have been down to any alcohol, for, anyone who drank as much as he had done, because after all it wasn't that much, yet the night before still seemed a distant memory. He continued to lie there, eyes closed and considered for a moment, it must have been one hell of a night though, but what if it was a nightmare I'd probably remember some part of it and what if anything could have caused this hangover he is suffering. Thoughts rolled about in his mind for a while but nothing would explain why he felt so much like shit. He had a real heavy head and could barely open his eyes. With an intake of air and grunt he would attempt to get up from his bed or from what he may think was his bed, still in his shirt and denim jeans and his favourite brown tassel shoes Jack Law soon realised that he must have been in a coma, he slumped back down on the sofa closed his eyes slowly but gently rubbed his brow then temple, grunting and breathing in deeply, but intentionally. Somehow he knew this type of massage was the only remedy available to him until his benign hangover passed away from him. As he lay on his back he thought a strong cup of coffee might help the situation, opening his left eye Jack made out a way across the room, it was a way that led to a kitchen through an archway, a kitchen upon the horizon just across what seemed like unkempt and untidy room. The state of the room took his mind off the much needed coffee, the walls were like a dark brown colour and the floor was wooden with a multicoloured yet dark rug that should be laid flat against the floor but it was not it was rippled across the middle, it had the appearance of being unstable like and very disturbed the more he looked around the more he realised that the room was unstable he saw the wall paper slowly stripping itself of the walls and bits of the decor just falling to the floor, revealing blackened and burnt embers, there was a side board up against the wall with a brown finish like walnut opposite a window, a curtain hung un-drawn where beyond its yellowed haze, offered little light into the room. It occurred to him how could he live like this, but what was that smell, his senses started to recover fully, he sat up and shrugged of that which was holding him down and spoke out.

'Where am I . . . What the hell time is it?'

'Why do you ask all these questions fool . . . don't you know'

He looked at his watch but the dim light was useless.

'Where the hell is I' he raised his voice. But the language he spoke was that of the dead, and he never saw the face in the watch and that it was of a black called Charles Johnson the face he saw in the wine glass.

He was wrong to have thought that he does not know the answers nor did he know how he found himself in that place.

'Too many questions you blabber . . . bring forth the too few answers to what we seek'.

'What the heck, now I, hearing voices and I talk to myself, what will thee beseech of men who do harm is this his forfeit, to be bound in a room which burns yet no fire exist only a fowl stench that curses me sinus, I fought hard with him and he fought hard with me also, the John struck a blow to my cranium after he saw me about his daughter, I but tendered to her wetted corpse on this very floor but she was really dead, I cried a muted forlorn sigh my blood was hot when I took the blow I reached high for a weapon, tis the lamp stand I found and struck thee back, Its fuel spilt out and caught John alight. First it was about his own head, like a match stick, his shoulders next, then to the floor he fell next to his daughter, the blaze ballooned about them both, I fear to say they were engulfed the fire amassed the bed clothes but my head burns but it was not by fire, the back of my head hurts me, what is wrong with my head, so much blood is on my hands, I am guilty so guilty of obsession, his wife I took as my own and now this fire burns like the passion which Grace Ruanple and I Charles Johnson felt for each other, hot and wanton, the room is burning oh Lord . . . Lord, the Gideon has fled the battle, I must leave this furnace, I have killed them both my God'.

Jack Law got to his feet and strolled over by the window and stood there, in his mind he sees the fire and imagined the scorching heat that was behind him and the burning room, but, he himself not touched by the heat of the blazing furnace, he then looked up and around about the curtain before uttering his observations.

'Lord, what hell is this. I suffer this fate as if it were my own, I prey oh God release me from this horror'

The curtain has not been opened for an era, the little remnants therein left too much to ponder and him to pace about, his own steps he heard as he sometimes brushed the sole of his shoes against the timbers, quite an eerie feeling came about like a breeze from an opening unknown, a feeling within a dead calm was there, but can a man be wondering about in a room filled by fire, either way, he raised his left hand to put about and cover his face as if to expect a probable clause to an event that will no doubt jump out and attack him. He put his right hand up and across his face also, then facing toward the left side of the curtain he took hold between his fingers then paused then he tugged once and again the curtain gave way releasing dust, debris and a burst of fire rushed in but it was only light a light unseen for many many days, the suddenness and calamitous nature of the opening gave fright to the man. And as the dust and light struck at the same time he was forced back from the window . . .

'Ugh! Shit fuck . . . ! He spluttered.

'Didn't expect to get covered in debris did you?' the walls spoke to him as it appeared he was not alone.

The dust started to clear and revealing the old woman as she was just a floating outside the window she was menacing with her greying locks billowing out behind her, real ghost like, her stare unfocused the eyes glazed black and opened wide but she was trying to look around the room but limited to only looking in through the window, evidently the ghost could not enter as she bumped into the glass like a fly, he was transfixed by the sight and blinded by the flash, he saw the old woman's ghost-like body limping like a banner in a low wind, a floating, the light which had blinded him was that which came out from the setting sun like a blade a fire, orange, the colour orange against the nimbus clouds a backdrop seen and admired from that very window many times by June Ruanple, the perfect view across the Wettersham Valley was seen and cherished toward the end of summer and the fall.

'Tell . . . before you are consumed my darling . . .'

The old ghost smirked and mocked him as he stood in awe she could not control her gape as dibble spilled off her bottom lip.

'The place you are in is my house, where be my lost child, and John?'

The ghost was that of June Ruanple.

Mrs Ruanple was denied access to the house after the fire the house was burnt to the ground and ever since that faithful day only the memory of it stood, the memory of the little house at the end of this path stood for the purpose of the locals, the fellows, the people that lived in the valley, they had their own ritual, they formed a pact and that pact they called it the . . . The Billet Society and lest we forget the pact that was formed, that demented forum that made up a secret then gave it up to be fondled, yhea the Higher Decree, Carl Mitten, an associate member of the Fellows and Shelia Charlise MCA EEc. Tim Watt MCA EEc (Given) and Judge Demus Trause, it was incumbent upon the Judge Demus Trause, so, he passed up the secrets to be fondled and everything that she had as possession apart from her tarnished garments about her supple frame was lost therein Aprils body was never found only the remains of Johns body was discovered along with that of a black man called Charles Johnson the forensics team found what they described as two males. Had they searched harder they would have discovered Aprils too but it was the closeness of her remains to her father's they missed it. Grace would have never believed for one moment that an affair with this man Charles Johnson could lead to such destruction. Jack Law and his own revelations near gave full truth to what had actually befallen her; she thought that her days of promiscuous fault with him had lead to her daughter to leave home.

It took a few days before the story reached the news papers and for Delia to become aware of the facts, the fact that her colleague Charles was dead and that she may be complicit in the travesty, she feared that the police may want to talk to her anytime soon; Grace Ruanple's daughter was missing the news story read.

It is the city glue that binds them but, really, Delia did not need to worry but she felt the guilt and she also had the original love letter that she thought was sent by Grace, she panicked and set up a meeting with the woman. Delia's intention was to hand the letter personally to Grace at least then it was not thrown away and she knows exactly where it is and if the police do come she could guide them without fear or cause and at least the owner has it back, the tonic was used up anyway. It would also give her the opportunity to look the woman Charles was seeing face to face typical of Delia she was a little insecure.

Delia arranged to meet with Grace at Rubies coffee shop of all places.

'Hello, are you Delia?' Grace walked in the coffee shop wearing dark glasses.

'Hi you must be Grace . . . Hi . . . please, take a seat, yes I am Delia, and please sit' Delia was gleeful welcoming and acted reassuringly.

'What is it that you want' Grace was abrupt but sat down but kept her glasses on.

'Oh my dear . . . I can see that you are still grieving the death of you're . . .'

Delia stopped she had just realised she was dealing with a woman that has just lost two lovers and she may have taken on more than she could chew.

'Oh I am sorry please forgive me how could I be so insensitive' she says and ask 'Would you like a coffee?'

Grace looked at Delia but couldn't work out why she turned uncomfortable.

'What is that you want do you have word about my daughter? I don't want anything just get to the point' Grace was impatient and ready to leave if the next word wasn't what she wanted to here.

Delia took out the letter from her hand bag then handed it to Grace, she was a little worried, Grace opened it, and Delia studied Grace as she looked at the letter, Grace became real angry and infused with rage and slapped Delia in the face. 'Where did you get this!?' she screamed out she had got up and stormed out. Delia had no time to respond even that worried look on her face was gone in an instant. Rubie looked over but she missed the action.

Delia was bruised and battered she got up and walked out also nothing else was said. 'God what a bad idea that was I'm sure glad that's over' she said feeling a might sorry.

The letter gave no comfort to Grace if anything it just added insult to her injury, she couldn't work out why her hand writing was forged even up to her signature, but it could only have been her daughter that did it, but why? Grace just couldn't work out why was her daughter would do that. Did she kill them both? I can see why she shot the guy in the back of the head but why would she burn her father? Was she in love with my lover . . . ? None of it made sense and most of all where is she. It was all too much to bear Mrs Grace Ruanple died of a broken heart a year later, exactly twelve months to the day and with much regret and sorrow, she believed that her loss of a marriage counsel and the love and affection of her only child; daughter April, was all due to the liaisons with Charles, her broken promise to her husband, the vows she had made when exchanged at the altar between man and woman . . . to love, honour and cherish . . . faithful . . . !. Mrs Grace Ruanple, allowed herself to be entangled with two lovers.

This gave rise to the spirited storm, true, the vexed nature that bloomed which is now in seasoned with the knowledge that April died at Jacks Laws revelation, had she ever known this when she was alive she would have murdered!, not for her own guilt but for, how could he take her child also, the word thundered through the window along with the blade of light that flickered when nimbus covered the sun. The curtain was torn down to exact his own revelation.

It was a real crisis for ghost of Grace Ruanple, her promiscuous fault was to blame for the fall of her fame, but she reviled in death and the death of her daughter, that she turned in her grave immensely she removed herself and was thrown down in shame, stricken from the society where she dwelt and became buried in an unnamed grave and her grieved spirit left to roam the earth and to remain thither about the little house at the end of this path.

Jack Law's vision continued but become blurred as the voices become ever stronger, he is beckoned to tell all by the ghost that looked into the room the ghost was denied to ever enter again that house but now that the curtain was taken away the spirit of Mrs Grace Ruanple was able to look inside a terrible accord was struck the agreement brought forth a rebuke from the other side the vile stench of burnt flesh opened up and the guilt re-entered the memory and he fell amidst the smouldering wreck with blood seeping out from a wound in the back of his head.

'No more please, no more I cannot take anymore of this, it is true they died at my hand, I . . . I am weakening . . . I truly loved his wife and April . . . I' Jack Law paused he took sight of his watch and barely made out the reflection on the watch face but it was not his face he saw but the face of a complete stranger. His eyes closed and he lay still.

Meanwhile . . .

'It is time for him to be delivered we have no further use of this earthling, turn him about that he return to his life, we have now seen what became of the woman and the reasons why she wanders about our realm and tis true Shelia Charlise that poor woman suffered for her cause but this time Tim Watt you near took it too far the power that you're given you must use wisely for too much strength we cannot afford no death to occur in our realm . . . Ah . . . Carl Manning you worry so, you forget Judge Demus Trause followed the human throughout this trial?'

'Not at all did you not hear for yourselves that at times through his trial consciousness near took him and thus near became himself, what say you Judge . . . Demus . . . the Trause, let us the fellows of the Billett Society stand as one and turn it back on him and release the hijacked mind of the earthling being'

'I Judge Demus Trause have split the cup that was sent up for the Higher Decree to manage the earthlings' sentence, thus, it was returned whole and so I declare, even though so close it came. In this our tabernacle and around this stump as we dare, I do declare that we required of one such that was indeed closer to the truth in manner and behaviour that one of our own should suckle him . . . Charlise bring back Deborah Winger'

'Ah, Beverly Parkson our fellow did truly fondle for the poor woman's cause, and true to the cause of Mrs Grace Ruanple and her lost innocence the child within her are now released, the Higher Decree chose Carl Manning'

'I Judge Demus the Trause turn him on a sixpence'

'Carl Mitten the associate member I order thee now to open the file marked confidential that is set before you and read the script that was fondled by the Higher Decree that we can forward to our outer reaches of our realm to debate again'

'The billet Society will meet in the boardroom of the Elite rooms the eve of the gala they will indeed orchestrate it they will deliver the lost child they will rake up the doting husband his spirit and remit them both to her and they will dwell amongst us about our realm as favour, and all because Grace Ruanple rue her woman's behaviour. So read I Carl Mitten from the file marked confidential'

Carl Mitten read like a true member of the society his oration was welcomed by the fellows as they sat surrounded by the great mahogany panels where elegant and tall book shelves filled with great works and historic precedence of past outcome, trials and tribulation past down by the Billett and its council. The boardroom panels open up to reveal many stars amongst a darkened blue sky like that of the dead of night. The fellows spoke to each other with righteous tones, noble like, and with great fortitude then filed out of the room dissipating into the blue.

'Hey . . . wake up . . . hey, wake up man you can't sleep hear this is a work place did you not sleep last night, wake up man wake up'

What is going on in here?' a woman walks in with a name tag Deborah Winger written on it.

'I have been trying to wake him up now about 15 minutes, he's like he is dead man but he is still breathing' says Jenny

'Turn that off' the woman with the name tag takes control and rest a hand on his shoulder, turn that music off'

'OK, he was working on this project with me and Mustafa and that bell sound he was trying to make it sound crystal clear, no shit'

'Just turn it off and up the lights for me. This guy is out of this world' the woman says. 'Jenny please stop the music . . . if you can call it that? And cut the bell out it is driving me mad and when you have done that please up the lights she' she demanded.

'Wow it is real cool in hear you feel that it is almost cold' says Mustafa

'He's waking up look at him he looks like he has seen a ghost, he looks like he has seen a ghost' Jenny says it twice

'What's up' he finally gets help and wobbled his head and says . . .

'Phew shit!'

'Are you ok CARL?' ask the woman with the name tag making sure he gets her name . . . My name Deborah would you like a coffee'

'Yes I am good, what's up guys I need that coffee'

'Here we go again says Jenny . . .'

End